"A brilliant, bold, and beautiful book. Lindsey Stoddard tackles tough, thorny topics with nuance and grace, never once compromising readability or relatability. She is the real deal."

—Author-illustrator **JARRETT LERNER**

"A book with real heart and real warmth; sure to be a real good addition to any bookshelf. This is a moving story about friendship, family, and the courage it takes to stand up to one's peers, a story that drew me right in and kept me absorbed until the last page. In a truthful, direct, and hard-hitting manner, Stoddard explores the cowardice of complicity, the pain of loss, the loneliness of guilt, and the cruelty of bullying. Like Reuben, this quiet book is an ode to strength of silence, as well as the power of words."

—**PADMA VENKATRAMAN**, Walter Award–winning author of *The Bridge Home*

"This genuinely thoughtful and ultimately joyful gem about friendship and the many ways that a voice has power is an absolute treasure. I was rooting for Gabe from the moment I met him and was captivated as he navigated his way through the small moments that have big meaning in middle school life, surprising himself along the way. *The Real Deal* is laced with humor and brimming with an abundance of heart— vibrant, charming, and absolutely real."

—**OLUGBEMISOLA RHUDAY-PERKOVICH**, author of *Operation Sisterhood*

The Real Deal

ALSO BY LINDSEY STODDARD

Just Like Jackie

Right as Rain

Brave Like That

Bea Is for Blended

THE REAL DEAL

LINDSEY STODDARD

HARPER

An Imprint of HarperCollins*Publishers*

Library of Congress Cataloging-in-Publication Data

Names: Stoddard, Lindsey, author.

Title: The real deal / Lindsey Stoddard.

Description: First edition. | New York : Harper, 2022. | Audience: Ages 8-12. | Audience: Grades 4-6. | Summary: Best friends Gabe and Oliver tackle family problems, bullying, and the challenge of dealing with the new kid in their sixth grade class, Reuben, who refuses to talk—and no one knows why.

Identifiers: LCCN 2021057321 | ISBN 978-0-06-320685-4 (hardcover)

Subjects: LCSH: Best friends—Juvenile fiction. | Friendship—Juvenile fiction. | Bullying—Juvenile fiction. | Secrecy—Juvenile fiction. | Families—Juvenile fiction. | Psychology—Juvenile fiction. | CYAC: Best friends—Fiction. | Friendship—Fiction. | Bullying—Fiction. | Family problems—Fiction. | Secrets—Fiction.

Classification: LCC PZ7.1.S7525 Re 2022 | DDC 813.6 [Fic]—dc23/eng/20220510

LC record available at https://lccn.loc.gov/2021057321

Typography by Sarah Nichole Kaufman and Catherine Lee

22 23 24 25 26   PC/LSCH   10 9 8 7 6 5 4 3 2 1

First Edition

For Kamahnie,
because you are the real deal.

"WHAT DO YOU MEAN he doesn't talk?" Chaz calls from the back of the room. "Like, ever? Why?"

Those are my questions too.

Ms. Leavitt says there are many reasons someone might not talk, but she doesn't have any answers for us. All she knows is that his name is Reuben, he'll be new to our class, and he doesn't speak. She says it like she's telling us something ordinary, like where he's from or what his favorite color is.

"We'll get to know him more tomorrow," she says.

"How?" Chaz asks.

That's exactly what I'm wondering too. This might be the first time I'm glad Chaz Gilbertson is in my class, so he can ask the questions that feel like things you shouldn't be asking.

"Through mind reading?" he continues. "Does he come with his own crystal ball or something?"

That gets Saunders and Orin laughing, and then the giggles start to spread, and even though Oliver's hiding his face behind one of my Dog Man books, I can tell he's snickering, too, because his shoulders are jumping up and down. And that gets me going because I'm imagining this new kid coming into class, pulling a crystal ball from his book bag, and setting it on the corner of his table with his notebook and pencil. I'm trying to hide my laugh in my hands, but I can't stop, and now the whole class is shaking.

Then Ms. Leavitt gives us a look. Her look. Which is not like any other teachers' looks. Theirs are *Don't you dare* looks, but Ms. Leavitt's is worse. Hers is an *Is that who you really are?* look.

And I'm pretty sure that *is* who Chaz really is. Someone who makes fun of a kid who doesn't talk.

Ms. Leavitt sends her look around the whole room, from Missy to Fiona to Lenny, until it's my turn and she looks me square in the eyes. "You can always tell if something is actually funny by how it feels in your guts," she tells us. "If you're doing that belly-aching-sore-muscles-makes-you-feel-free kind of laugh, then you know it's good-funny," she says. "But if you laugh and then it feels like you swallowed gobbledygook, you know it's not."

I cross my arms over my stomach and wish I could take back my laugh about the nontalking new kid and his crystal ball. I guess there aren't any benefits to having Chaz Gilbertson in my class after all, because if he hadn't been saying all that stuff, we wouldn't have been laughing, and Ms. Leavitt wouldn't be giving us her look and making me feel all gobbledygooky.

She taps her fingers gently on the table in front of her and says, "That's why people say, *Follow your gut.*"

Everyone has stopped laughing, and it's silent for a few moments. A few uncomfortable moments. So I stare at my hands.

But then Ingrid whispers a question: "Where's he from?" And a hundred more follow.

"What's he like?"

"Does he use sign language?"

"Never talks? Like, ever in his whole life? Or did he just kind of quit?"

"Who quits talking?"

Ms. Leavitt says, again, that she doesn't have any answers. She also says that when we were entering her class at the beginning of the school year, she didn't have much information about us, either, and she preferred it that way, to meet us herself and see what we wanted to share.

Then she looks right over the tops of her glasses one more time, and into all our eyes, and says, "We will welcome Reuben into our community when he arrives tomorrow."

I nod when her eyes meet mine.

"Moving on, then," she says, and hands us the directions for our next English project. They're printed on skinny slips of paper, and there are only two points listed for the whole assignment:

Create something that tells a story.

Due Wednesday, April 18.

Everyone shoots their hand in the air, including me. I want to know if we can make a comic. And if we can, I want to know if we can work with partners, because Oliver's way better at drawing than I am, but I'm the storyteller.

Everyone's calling out questions like, *How long should it be?* and *What kind of story? Does it have to be true?*

I can tell Ms. Leavitt is listening, but instead of answering anything, she says, "Why don't you read over the directions with a partner and chat about your ideas." As if that's going to help us at all.

I turn to Oliver. "What do you think?"

"I don't know," he says, and leans in a little closer to me. "But I got a message from my uncle Toby last night, and he says I can invite a friend on our backpacking trip this summer."

"Oh," I whisper, and tap my pencil eraser on the table. "So, who are you going to invite?" I ask, because even though Oliver and I have been best friends since pre-K, I'm not sporty like he is.

I'm the kind of kid who gets book-tans across my lower arms from sitting out in the sun and reading all summer, which is pretty far from the kind of kid who backpacks for four days, three nights, and thirty-five miles on the Appalachian Trail with his Vermont-forest-ranger uncle.

Oliver laughs and says, "Oh, come on. Please?"

I sit up a little straighter in my seat and say, "You want *me* to go?"

"*You* are my best friend," he says.

I want to say yes, because he's my best friend, too, but I also don't want our friendship to melt on the side of the trail in a puddle of my own sweat and tears.

Then Chaz walks by on the way to the pencil sharpener and taps Oliver on the shoulder. "Three-on-three at recess?" he whispers.

Oliver nods and says, "Yeah. Meet you on the court."

And then I start imagining Oliver inviting Chaz into the woods with him and Uncle Toby, and them coming back and talking about all the adventures they had on the trail, and it makes me think maybe I could keep up with Oliver on this one. I might never be able to steal a basketball from him on the playground court at recess, but who can't walk in the woods with a backpack on?

"I'll ask my mom," I say. Oliver smiles and throws his arm around my shoulders even though we both know that this does not make it a sure thing, because my mom's one hundred times more protective than his mom. She didn't even let me start riding my bike to school by myself until the beginning of this year. Sixth grade. And if I don't text her as soon as I get here, she calls the school, and Ms. Phillips announces, over the loudspeaker, that I need to come to the office to call my mother.

If I had some brothers or sisters maybe Mom could spread all that worry out. Oliver has three older sisters, and his mom started letting him ride his bike to school in second grade. But all my mom's worry goes straight to me.

The bell rings, and Ms. Leavitt says we'll start making plans for our projects tomorrow. I still have a hundred questions, but I pack up my book bag and head out the door.

Later, in math class, Oliver finishes the Dog Man book beneath our table and hands it back to me.

"So good," he whispers.

"New one is out today," I whisper back.

And right when the spine of the book hits my hand beneath our table, I get the best idea ever for Ms. Leavitt's project. We could create a comic with a new character, one that's part Oliver and part me, like some kind of sporty-bookish-crime-fighting hero, and it's all Oliver and I can talk about through math class and lunch.

But then, when we're getting ready for recess, I hear everyone chattering about the new kid again, the kid who doesn't speak. They're making up stories about why someone would do that, just not talk, not ever.

"Maybe he was born without a tongue."

"Or he was kidnapped as a baby and put in an underground prison and they just rescued him and he's never even heard words before and Ms. Leavitt will have to teach him the alphabet."

"Or a witch cast a spell on him and until he kisses someone in our class he'll be trapped without speech."

Everyone says *Ewwww* and then Chaz says, "He's probably just stupid."

He kind of spits out that last word, *stupid*, because sometimes Chaz is plain mean. Teachers never really catch him, either, because his mom had him take this test in kindergarten to find out that he's "gifted." I guess when you're "gifted" you get away with things. I don't know about all that advanced and genius stuff, but I do know that Chaz gets good grades, teachers always call on him, he gets a thousand cool points every day by making kids laugh, and he barely ever gets in trouble.

Ms. Leavitt is the first teacher who isn't like that. She doesn't call on him if his hand isn't raised, and she doesn't make him her classroom assistant, and if she hears him being terrible, she tells him to quit it.

We're walking through the big doors from the lunchroom to the playground, and my mind is running a hundred miles per hour thinking about a secret underground prison and wondering how people even learn to talk anyway. And it makes me think of a project I did in third grade on worms, and before I know it, I'm saying, "Did you know that worms communicate by touch and taste? And they can feel vibrations from deep in the earth."

When I say it, I'm thinking that would be a cool superhero talent to have, but Orin immediately scrunches his nose and goes, "Ewww! Do you think the new kid lives in mud?"

And then Chaz blurts out, "Wormboy!" and wiggles his body around the hall. Everyone starts to laugh because when he's not being just plain mean, he's being sideways-mean, which usually comes out as sounding kind of funny at first.

I think I'm the only one not laughing, which feels

weird, so I let out a little chuckle, but I'm paying too much attention to my guts now after what Ms. Leavitt told us, and they're starting to feel like gobbledygook.

I try to say, "No, that's not what I meant," but everyone's snickering and nudging me like that was a good one, and as soon as we get to the recess yard, we all split up and run to play, and it's too late.

So I tell myself it's not a big deal. Then I pull on my sweatshirt and find a spot on the grass that isn't wet, against the trunk of a tree by the playground, to work on our new comic character. Oliver joins the basketball game.

Tonya is pushing Missy and Jade on the tire swing, and Andre is chasing Fiona across the jungle gym. They slide on a puddle of slush down the ramp toward the monkey bars, and it looks like they're skating on their sneakers, flapping their arms and giggling. The recess aide blows her whistle and gestures for them to slow down. They've been strict about no running on the jungle gym after a playground accident that happened a few towns from here when I was in fourth grade. We all quit running when we heard about it, but now sometimes we forget, until we hear the whistle. Andre and Fiona stop quick, then swing off the monkey bars and walk to the gazebo.

Then I hear an *ohhhhh* from the basketball court,

and Oliver is standing beneath the hoop, where he missed a shot. "Better work on your game or we're going to have to replace you with Wormboy," Saunders says, and it sends Orin laughing.

And now that I'm listening, I can hear *Wormboy* flying around the playground until everyone is saying it, and the gobbledygook in my guts is growing.

2.

AFTER SCHOOL, I PEDAL fast to the bookstore, partly because the new Dog Man book is out and I can't wait to see it on the shelves, and partly because I'm thinking maybe if I ride fast enough, the wind will blow the memory of *Wormboy* right out of my mind. Every time I think about it, I get a wave of gobbledygook.

I leave my bike next to Mom's in the rack outside and clip my helmet on the strap of my book bag. As I walk up the steps, I'm trying to come up with the best way to ask her about the backpacking trip.

I could just mention it casually, like point to a hiking guide on one of the shelves in the store and say, *Oh, by the way, I've been meaning to ask you* . . . like it's not a big deal so of course she'd let me go.

Or maybe I should wait and ask Dad. He's sometimes easier to get a yes out of, but Dad's a nurse who works late at the hospital, and even though he should still be sleeping at seven o'clock when I'm eating breakfast, he sets an alarm so we can eat Corn Pops together, then goes back to sleep when I leave for school. And I don't want to fill our groggy, early-morning cereal time arguing about whether I should be able to hike in the woods with my best friend.

When I walk into the store, Liv is helping a customer in the middle grade section. She sees me and nods toward the new arrivals shelf, and I nearly fall right over when I see at least a dozen of the new Dog Man books all lined up. I take one in my hands and I love how it feels, just like all the others in the series, a hardcover but without the dust jacket sliding around and getting in the way, and heavier than it looks because the pages are thick with drawings.

I can hear Mom on the phone with a customer, searching for an order, so I take my time looking at the book. I even fan the pages and take a quick smell, because not everyone knows this, but new-book smell is right up there with brownies-in-the-oven smell.

Mom lets me pick a new book from the store on the first day of every month. We make it this entire celebration, too, where we get ice cream and I read the rest of the night. That's one of the cool things about Mom. But today is April third, and I just picked out *Haylee and Comet* two days ago. So I know there's no chance of getting this Dog Man book today.

Then I hear Liv say to her customer, "You know what? This sounds like a question for Gabe." She looks over at me, and I give a little wave.

"That's me," I say. "I'm Gabe."

She points to the man and says, "His niece is in fifth grade and loved all the Diary of a Wimpy Kid books. What do you think she should read next?"

This is why I love coming to the bookstore. Because I might not have many cool points, but when it comes to reading, I've got all the points in the world, and if I were older than eleven, I would work here and run the children's section no problem.

"She should try *Smile* and *Invisible Emmie*," I say. I look at Liv and stroke my pretend beard like I'm thinking. "Then *Haylee and Comet* and *Real Friends*. And obviously, Dog Man." I wave the copy I'm holding in front of me like it's saying hello.

Liv nods and looks back at her customer. "You've heard it from our resident expert." He laughs and says that's good enough for him, and Liv shows him where to find the books.

I peek toward the front desk, and my mom smiles

and gives me the *one-minute* sign. She thanks her customer and says the order should arrive next week, and when she puts down the phone, I hold up the Dog Man book and smile my best pretty-please smile.

I know she'll say no, but that's my plan; I want to get a couple of noes out of her before I ask about the backpacking trip. Maybe she'll be more likely to say yes after a few noes.

"It's not even close to May first," she reminds me, but before I can reshelve the graphic novel she says, "Oh, what the heck? I'll give you an advance for this one," and reaches out for the book.

"It's OK, Mom. You don't have to. . . ."

But she just snaps her fingers and says, "Hand it over."

And there goes my plan. It's like she has some kind of sixth sense and knows that I'm going to ask for something bigger later, and she better say yes to the book so she can feel good about the no she's saving up.

I hand over the Dog Man and say, "Thanks, Mom," because I really do want the book. But then I add, "I really appreciate when you say yes."

She looks at me funny and says, "You're welcome, hon . . . Gabe." She's trying her best not to call me *honey* in public. So far her best has not been that great.

Mom puts the book on the counter, and Eva, the

owner, rings us up. Mom pays for the book, and I slide it into my bag.

Then Liv's customer steps up to the cash register with an armful of books. I give him a thumbs-up, and on our way out, Liv smiles and says, "Happy trails," which makes me think of all the arguments Oliver told me after school to prove to Mom that the backpacking trip will be safe and that I won't be eaten by a bear or mauled by a moose.

We pull our bikes off the rack, and Mom leads. She makes an exaggerated left-turn hand signal at the intersection while I run through Oliver's points in my head.

One: The Appalachian Trail is marked by white blazes painted on the trees, plus we have maps and a guidebook, so it'd be impossible to get lost.

Two: There's only one type of venomous snake in Vermont, the timber rattlesnake, and it's endangered. This one I looked up on my phone because if I knew there were going to be a whole bunch of venomous snakes slithering around my hiking boots, I'd be the first to tell Oliver I couldn't go and blame it on my mom. Garter snakes are creepy enough.

And three: Oliver's uncle Toby works for the Department of Forests, Parks, and Recreation, so he knows everything you need to know about navigating trails, and first aid, and slinging your food bag up in a tree so bears don't rip down your tent looking for it.

We ride single file up the street, and Mom throws some questions over her shoulder. "How was school?"

I get a pang right in the gobbledygooks when I think about the new kid and how *Wormboy* is inching its way around the whole grade, but I just say, "Good."

"Did you read anything cool? Write anything cool?"

"Yeah," I say, and I actually want to tell her about the project in English and the new character for our comic, but I'm also biking uphill, so I can only really get out one-word answers.

We make a full stop at the one red light in town. "Can't wait to hear more," she says. Then the light changes to green, and we turn up the last hill to home and coast into our driveway.

After we park our bikes in the garage, Mom grabs a shovel and starts hacking at the last bit of the slushy fort that Oliver and I made over winter break, when there was perfect packing snow. Then the whole thing turned to solid ice, and we used it as a slide for the rest of the winter, and now it's the last thing in our yard to melt. Today is sunny, and Mom is determined.

I grab one of the plastic lawn chairs in the garage and put it right in the driveway facing the sun. I'm just taking out the new Dog Man book when Mom unzips her fleece and tosses it on the front step. "Don't you think you should give Puppy some exercise?"

Puppy is my hamster.

When I begged Mom to take me to the pet store last year, she told me I could choose between a fish and a hamster. I walked her by the fluffy puppies yelping at me to buy them, and she said, "We're not getting a puppy, Gabe."

"But Andre from my class got a puppy," I told her.

"And it's chewing Andre's sneakers and peeing on Andre's floor and jumping up on Andre's counter to eat Andre's lunch," she said.

So I picked a hamster because at least it has fur and named it Puppy because I was still mad.

"Let's see how you do with this hamster first," Mom said. "A pet is a lot of responsibility."

I put my book down on the chair and go inside to get Puppy. My room smells a little like those wood shavings we use to line the bottom of her cage and a little like the hamster pee they're soaking up.

"Come on, Puppy," I say, and coax her out of her rock-cave hideout with my finger. I cup her in my hands, drop her in the clear plastic exercise ball, secure the little door on top, and say, "Time for a workout."

The last bits of our fort are scattered around the yard and melting fast when I get back outside. I put Puppy down on the driest part of the lawn and jog a few steps to see if she'll follow me. She reaches up and motors her little paws until the ball starts rolling. I loop around our birch tree, hoping she'll chase me, but she crashes right into the trunk. Then she rolls back a little, starts over, and crashes into it again.

I sigh and wipe a little smudge of mud off the ball, then help her around the tree. I'm thinking how ridiculous I must look running around my yard with a plastic ball, and how much more fun this would be with an actual puppy.

I give up and let her roam the yard in the ball while I sit back down with Dog Man. Mom grabs another lawn chair from the garage and sets it next to mine. "Make sure Puppy doesn't roll into the street," she says.

"I would never let that happen," I say. "I'm really responsible."

Mom nods. "So tell me about school."

I skip the part about the new kid and start in on Ms. Leavitt's project.

"I hope we can work in partners because Oliver and I want to make our own graphic novel kind of like Dog Man," I tell her. "Except instead of a half-dog, half-policeman character, it would be a half-Gabe, half-Oliver character, and we'd go around solving all these crimes where we have to be super sporty and super bookish."

Mom laughs. "Now, that's creative," she says.

And as I'm explaining the project, I realize this is a good time to ask her about the backpacking trip. "I really hope Ms. Leavitt lets us partner up," I say. "Because Oliver's my best friend. And it's important for friends to work together and go on adventures. Don't you think?"

Mom gives me a funny look and says, "Of course."

Now's the exact best time to ask, but at that very moment I hear Puppy's plastic ball drop off the curb and roll into the street. It falls hard enough to crack open the little door on top, and even though I get up fast and run to show Mom how responsible I am, I'm not fast enough, because Puppy's found the exit, and I'm thanking my lucky stars there aren't any cars coming as she scurries across the street and into our neighbor's driveway.

Her little paws move one hundred miles per hour, and Mom is screaming, "Gabe! Get her!"

And I'm thanking my lucky stars again that Puppy stops to sniff a leaf because I get there before she can dart into the Hendersons' garage, which is so full of stuff we'd never find her.

"Well, that was a close one," Mom says. She's picking up the plastic ball and inspecting it for any cracks.

"Yeah." I carry Puppy back across the street. "They should make those exercise balls more durable," I say.

Mom holds it out to me, and I drop the hamster in. She snaps the little door shut. "Pets require a lot of responsibility," she reminds me.

When we sit at the counter for dinner Mom looks at her watch, and I know she's wondering if Dad is on a break and if he's getting something to eat too. Dad has had this new late shift for the whole school year, but we're still not used to him missing dinner.

"You know," Mom says. "If Ms. Leavitt decides you can't work in pairs for the project, you could still create that comic with Oliver. It would be a fun adventure." She twirls her fork and winds up a bite of spaghetti.

I nod. "Yeah, I bet we will."

Mom nods, and I take a breath, and I know that if I don't ask now the conversation will circle back to Puppy rolling into the road and how irresponsible I am.

"Speaking of friendship and adventures and working together and stuff," I say.

Mom raises her eyebrows.

"Can I go backpacking this summer with Oliver and his uncle Toby?"

She presses her lips together, and I know she's trying to think of an around-the-side way of saying no.

"You know that's kind of a big deal, right?" she asks.

I nod, and I'm pretty sure she's thinking that I'm not

nearly sporty enough. "I can do it, Mom," I say. "I walk with my book bag full of stuff all the time."

Mom laughs and pats my arm. "A backpacking trip isn't like walking down the hallway in school," she says. Then she puts down her fork and looks me right in the eyes. "If this is something you want to do, you'll have to show some real responsibility first." She glances toward Puppy, who is now happily rolling around the living room in her plastic ball, and I give her a look like *Puppy spinning down the street like a bowling ball has nothing to do with this.* "You'll have to learn a few things about being in the woods," she says.

"I'll check out some books from the library," I tell her. "Guides and maps and first-person accounts from super-hikers."

She laughs again and says, "You also need to actually go in the woods, Gabe. Get some exercise, try it out, see what it's like."

I nod and say, "OK."

"Wasn't there a packet you brought home at the beginning of the year with a list of after-school clubs? I wonder if there's an outdoorsy one you could join."

"Club?" I say. I'm not a club kid.

There's a bit of silence as Mom reaches for the Parmesan cheese. I pick up my fork and twirl another bite of spaghetti.

"I'm pretty sure we recycled that packet," I say. "Plus, all the clubs are probably already full. They started in September."

Mom takes a sip from her glass and says, "You better check."

"So your answer about the backpacking trip is . . ."

She looks at me. "Maybe."

3.

WHEN WE GET TO school the next day, everyone's whispering about the new kid again and wondering where he is, but no one's calling him Wormboy. They've moved on to Silent Sucker and Mute Button and a bunch of other names I didn't come up with, and it makes me feel relieved, but then kind of rotten for feeling relieved. Paying attention to my guts is not easy.

When Oliver sees me coming, he puts out his fist for a bump and says, "What'd your mom say?"

"She didn't say no," I tell him, and we connect knuckles. "But she did say I have to spend more time in the woods first." Oliver nods like that's not a bad idea. "I might have to join an outdoorsy club."

He laughs and says, "Gabe in a nature club?"

"The things I do for you," I say.

He smiles and looks around for Principal Tacker. Then he pulls out his phone. "Uncle Toby sent me this map of our route. . . ."

I lean into him to see, but I'm also looking out for Principal Tacker because she has some kind of sixth sense about cell phones. Kids call her Principal *Taker* because by the end of the day she has a drawer full of phones. Some kids call her Principal *Tattler*, too, because she calls home to tell on you, then demands that a grown-up comes to school to pick up the phone.

My phone's never been taken.

Neither has Oliver's until exactly this second because Principal Tacker swings open the doors to the yard, and I'm following her gaze to Oliver's hand, which isn't moving fast enough to zip open his book bag.

"Mr. Quick," she says. That's Oliver's last name, and it fits him perfectly except for right now. Her voice cuts through all the commotion, and she sticks out her open palm like she's saying *Hand it over.*

"Oh, come on! The bell hasn't even rung. . . ."

"Mr. Quick," she repeats. "No phones on school grounds."

"Principal Tacker, it was my fault. I asked him to show me—" I start to say, but she cuts me right off and tells Oliver he has five seconds. She waves her fingers like she doesn't have time for our excuses.

Oliver hangs his head, steps toward her, and puts the phone in her hand.

She wraps her fingers around it and says, "I'll be alerting your mom about this," then turns back into the building.

"Sorry," I say.

But he just shakes his head and says, "Tattler. I can't believe she's going to call my mom."

"I bet the hiking route is really great," I say, but I can't cheer him up right now, and that feels pretty rotten, too, so I just press my shoulder into his shoulder, which means *This is rotten, but I got you.*

When I look up I see Saunders point to a page in Chaz's open notebook. "I vote yes," he says, and Chaz makes a mark on the page.

"What's that for?" Oliver asks, and Chaz tells us about the bet they have going and how it's split down the middle. Half the class thinks Ms. Leavitt will be able to get the silent new kid to talk by the end of the day; the other half thinks she won't.

Andre comes up and says, "Count me in for no."

Chaz looks up at Oliver and me. "Place your bets."

Oliver shrugs and so do I. Then the bell rings, so Chaz zips his notebook in his book bag, and I'm glad I didn't have time to vote, but I'm also thinking I'd say yes. Because Ms. Leavitt is everyone's favorite teacher, so if anyone could get him to talk, it'd be her.

When we get to Ms. Leavitt's room, there's still no sign of the new kid.

She comes out to the hallway and says, "Good morning," and gives us fist bumps as we enter. Like I said, Ms. Leavitt's cool. And even though she has that look that makes you get back to work before it burns a hole right through you, she'd also never take a phone, or send you to Principal Tacker's office, or call your family to complain. "When you're in my classroom," she says, "you're my business." And she means it. Because it's already April and she still hasn't sent anyone to the office.

We're all inside the room and waiting, but Ms. Leavitt is still in the hall, and when she comes in, she's with the new kid. But I'm thinking this might not be Reuben at all because he's tall and has brown hair and jeans and sneakers and looks like he could just open his mouth any second and say, "Hey, everyone, what's up?"

But he just smiles and walks to the table near the classroom library and sits.

I'm trying not to stare at him, but it's hard. I want to see if there's anything else about him that looks different or seems off, but he pulls a notebook and pencil from his book bag and faces toward the front of the room. Ms.

Leavitt says she's excited to welcome Reuben to our class and that she's going to do attendance out loud today so he can begin to learn our names.

"When you hear your name raise your hand and say *here*," she tells us. "Like it's the first week of school."

Orin and Saunders laugh because they voted yes and now Reuben's going to have to raise his hand and say *here*, and they'll win the bet.

"Cass Bennett," Ms. Leavitt says.

"Here," Cass says, and raises her hand. Reuben looks over at Cass's table and nods.

"Lenny Daviano."

"Here."

When she gets to me I raise my hand and say, "Here," and when Reuben looks at me, I smile and wave, which makes Chaz laugh and mumble, "He can *hear* you," under his breath, which gets Saunders and Orin laughing too. But Ms. Leavitt gives them that look, and they shut their mouths, and she moves on.

"Oliver Quick."

"Here."

Everyone's moving to the edge of their seats because we're getting toward the end of the alphabet, and we all want to know if Reuben will say *here*.

Then Ms. Leavitt looks up from her attendance

sheet, smiles, and says, "And we all know Reuben Tanner is here. Reuben, we're so glad you've joined us," and checks off his name.

Then she just moves on to Fiona Watson.

There's a huge gasp and I'm part of it. I gasp so big, just like everyone else in class does, from Cass Bennett to Fiona Watson.

"That's it?" Chaz says.

Ms. Leavitt looks at him over her glasses. "Yes, that's everyone," she says.

"But . . ."

"Yes, Chaz, everyone is here." Then she looks out over all of us. "Who thinks they could explain *Moment of Meditation* to Reuben?"

No hands go up.

And I'm not sure if my guts are working, because I'm not laughing, but they're starting to feel gobbledygooky anyway, and before I know it, I'm raising my hand slowly.

I turn toward Reuben and say, "*Moment of Meditation* is five minutes of anything you want in your notebook."

Then Reuben raises his eyebrows, and I think he's trying to ask me something, and I think it's *Really? Anything?* because that's what I said when Ms. Leavitt first explained it at the beginning of the year. I'm not sure if that's what he's actually asking, but I answer anyway.

"Yeah," I say. "Anything." Then I think I must be nervous because I keep talking. "There aren't any rules," I say. "It's five minutes. It's in your notebook. It's your choice. Ms. Leavitt never gave us more directions than that. And on the first day everyone just wrote what they did over the summer, but by the second week we were all doing different things."

Reuben nods like that's really awesome, and it *is* really awesome.

I want to tell him that Andre always writes poetry and Chaz spent almost a month just tracing his hands and turning them into turkeys, which doesn't seem very "gifted" to me, and Fiona designs dresses, and Cass usually copies down her favorite song lyrics, and Ms. Leavitt never tells any of us that we're doing it wrong.

Reuben raises both eyebrows into a question. A question for me.

"I usually make comics," I say.

Reuben nods again and smiles.

Ms. Leavitt thanks me and sets her timer for five minutes. "So, let's begin."

There's a murmur about how Ms. Leavitt's not even trying to get him to talk, and some people want to change their votes, and Chaz is asking me if I'm some kind of silent-kid mind reader or something. I pretend I don't hear him, but I want to say that that's not it at all, and that it actually wasn't so hard to figure out what he might be trying to say, and that it felt pretty regular to just talk to him.

I look over toward Reuben's table and try to peek at what he's starting in his notebook. He's got his arm blocking the page, and I can't see without making it obvious, so I start in on my own.

I draw a circle on the blank page. It's supposed to be a picture of Puppy's exercise ball. Then I sketch a stick figure hamster inside it and stretch a speech balloon up from her mouth and write, *It's not easy living in a bubble.*

When we get to two and a half minutes, Ms. Leavitt looks up from her own paper and whispers, "This is halftime."

Halftime is when Oliver and I switch notebooks so he can make my sketches look more realistic and I can add some text to his drawings. I slide my notebook over, and he makes my circle look like an actual ball, fattens up poor stick figure Puppy, and adds whiskers.

"There," he says. Then he draws another frame with the same clear exercise ball, but this time there's a little drawing of me inside.

I smile, pull my notebook back, add a speech balloon coming up from my mouth, and write *I know how you feel, Puppy.* That makes us laugh, a good laugh, because we both know that if my mom could put me in a bubble she really might.

Ms. Leavitt gets up and walks through our tables to check in on how everyone is doing. When she gets to us, she whispers, "Good morning."

Oliver shrugs.

"Care to share?" she asks.

"Principal Tacker took my phone."

"Oh," Ms. Leavitt says. "Well, that is most unfortunate." But she doesn't say it like *Maybe you shouldn't have had your phone out, young man.* She says it like *That really stinks.*

I look over to Reuben's table again, but I still can't see his notebook, and then the timer goes off and Ms. Leavitt is telling us to find a good stopping place. When she passes by Reuben's table she hands him the slip of paper with the directions for our project, and I watch him read it. His face changes with the same questions we all had yesterday.

Ms. Leavitt calls for our attention and says, "I've thought about your questions for the project. And I think all of them are answered right here in the directions, except maybe one." Everyone is quiet, waiting.

And then right there, in the middle of the silence, Reuben hiccups. Loud.

No one knows what to do until Chaz bursts out laughing and says, "He speaks!"

Then everyone else bursts out laughing, and I do, too, and it feels good at first, because my laugh gets buried in with all of theirs.

But then I see Reuben's face get red, and I don't know if he's embarrassed or frustrated or mad or all those things together, but it shuts me right up because gobbledygook sneaks in fast.

Ms. Leavitt gives us her look and takes Chaz in the hallway, and when they come back Chaz slinks into his chair, and Ms. Leavitt's shaking her head like she's disappointed in everyone. Disappointed in me.

"What I was saying," she says, "is that you may work with partners if you wish."

Oliver and I pump our fists under the table.

"That's it," she says. "You can get to work."

At least ten hands shoot up, and kids aren't even waiting to be called on before they blurt out more questions. *Can it really be anything? Can I just draw? What if I don't have any stories?*

Ms. Leavitt gestures for us to put our hands down. "Trust me," she says. "You have everything you need to do this project." And I know that's all she's going to say.

I look over at Reuben quickly and try to give him a

sorry face, but he looks away fast and doesn't let me.

It's really loud for the first bit of work time, because everyone's trying to find a partner or figure out what the heck story they're supposed to be telling and how. But there are a few kids who get right to work.

Reuben's studying the directions with his forehead all scrunched up. Then he taps his fingers on the table like he's thinking.

Oliver grabs some plain white paper from the art shelves to start our new comic idea. In the first Dog Man book there's a big explosion, and in order to save them, a doctor sews Police Officer McKinley's body to Greg the dog's head. Together they make this heroic, crime-solving super-detective character named Dog Man. In our comic, the main character will be half Oliver and half me.

I tap my pencil on the top of the paper. "Oli-gabe?" I suggest. "Gabe-iver?"

"Yes! That's it! Gabiver," he says. So I write it on the top.

I scooch closer to Oliver until we're squished together shoulder to shoulder, and we spend the rest of the period trying to decide if we should have Oliver be the top half of the character, with his brown curly hair and nose-and-cheek freckles, or me with my dimples and square-framed glasses. In the end we decide we're going to change it up and draw the line right down the middle from head to toe instead.

The left side of Gabiver will be Oliver, and the right side will be me, which is perfect because Oliver's a lefty and I'm a righty.

Ms. Leavitt peers over my shoulder and smiles at the first sketch of our Gabiver character. His left side is wearing a sports jersey, shorts, and a high-top sneaker; has brown curly hair and a blue eye; and is holding a basketball. The right side has on jeans, a T-shirt, and one flip-flop; carries a book in his hand; and has straight brown hair, a dimpled cheek, and a square glasses frame over a brown eye.

I take out the Dog Man book to show Ms. Leavitt where we got the idea of mashing ourselves together into a character.

"In the book there's this officer . . . ," I start.

"Oh, please," she says. "Who doesn't know Dog Man? I just got the latest one for the classroom, but I'm reading it first." Then she moves on to the next group. Like I said, Ms. Leavitt is cool.

Oliver whispers with me about Gabiver in the rest of our classes, and he even sits out from basketball at recess to find a dry patch of ground for brainstorming ideas.

"He has to be a hero," Oliver says. "He has to solve some crime or figure out some mystery. Like in the real Dog Man."

Oliver looks around the playground like the answer might be out there somewhere. Saunders, Lenny, and Jolene are taking free throws on the court. Fiona is spinning Jade and Andre in fast circles on the tire swing. And Reuben is standing as far from the playground as possible. He's pressed back against the brick wall of the school building. Watching.

"I've got it," Oliver says. "The mystery of why Reuben doesn't talk."

I kind of shrug it off. Then I look at him because I'm not sure if he's serious.

"We can't actually do that," I say. "I mean, we have to hand it in to Ms. Leavitt and share it with the class."

"I know. I'm just kidding." And I'm relieved when he says that because Reuben's only been here for half a day and he's already got a ton of stories. Wormboy. Mute Button. Rescued from an underground prison. He's weird. He's stupid. He's rude.

I watch Reuben press into the bricks and shade his eyes with his hands.

Before the recess bell rings, we decide we'll start our story when Oliver and I first met in real life. Then there will be some big, exciting collision scene where Oliver hurts his right side and I hurt my left, and the nurse will have to save our lives by stitching us together down the middle. And then, together, as Gabiver, we'll be heroic and save a life or catch a criminal. That part we still have to figure out.

At the end of the day, I tell Oliver I have to go to the office to get my mom paperwork for clubs. He gives me a fist bump goodbye and goes to get changed for his own club, Sports Club. Then I look out the big glass windows from the lobby and see Reuben walking to the rack. He pulls off the bike right next to mine, then pedals down the sidewalk toward the road.

In the office I ask Ms. Phillips if she has the registration packet for after-school clubs.

"Thinking of joining?" she asks.

I nod, and she hands the papers to me. "I circled the ones with openings. One of your parents can sign the last page, and you can return it tomorrow."

I thank her and read down the list. One called Nature Club is circled, and I'm not surprised there isn't a wait-list for walking-in-the-woods-for-an-hour-after-school-instead-of-going-home club.

"They meet Monday, Wednesday, Friday," Ms. Phillips says. I nod, even though I think three days a week for the rest of the school year is a little excessive to prepare for one backpacking trip.

When I reach to zip the paperwork into my book bag, the office door flies open and in walks Principal Tacker with a tall girl who has short sticky-uppy light brown hair and a colorful bandanna folded over her head and tied behind her neck. She's not in sixth grade, because I know all the sixth graders.

"Get Rae Hendriks's mom on the phone," Principal Tacker says, and Ms. Phillips clicks on her computer and leans toward the screen.

"Go ahead and call her," the girl says. "She'll tell you I'm not going to any detention, and that's the truth." Then she slumps down hard in the plastic chair next to the office plant in the corner and crosses her arms over her chest.

I accidentally make eye contact, and her face is hard and annoyed, but then she actually kind of smiles and looks me up and down and says, "What'd you do?"

"N-nothing," I say.

"Oh," she says. "Boring."

4.

REUBEN

IT'S NOT THAT I can't talk.

5.

THAT NIGHT AT DINNER I put the paperwork for clubs on the counter in front of Mom. "Nature Club has openings," I say.

Mom smiles, then takes out her own list and slides it across to me.

1. Fancy hiking pack
2. Fancy water-bladder-holder thing
3. Fancy hiking socks (x4)

"I talked to Oliver's mom," she says. "Toby has a tent and an extra hiking sleeping bag, a water filtration system, and first aid. But we'll have to go shopping for these things if you're going to survive out there."

"Does this mean your maybe turned into a yes?"

"Under one condition," she says.

"OK." I'm waiting for her to say that she's coming too. That we're going to get matching hiking packs, share a fancy water-bladder-holder thing, and sleep head to toe in our own tent, but she doesn't.

She says, "You have to stick with Nature Club. Three days a week for the rest of the year. No quitting, because when you're out there in the woods, you can't quit on Oliver."

I jump up and give her a big hug and say "OK" because I would never quit on Oliver and I'm so happy she's not making herself my own personal hiking chaperone.

"It's a deal, then," she says. "But what will I do without you on those Nature Club afternoons?" She pulls me into another hug. "I guess more time in nature for you, more time in the bookstore for me."

"OK. Now I'm jealous," I say, and we both laugh. But I actually kind of *am*. Because I'm not sure sleeping in the woods and filtering your water so you don't puke your guts out sounds more fun than recommending titles to customers and opening big boxes of new arrivals.

The next morning, I hear Dad's alarm go off through the wall, and two minutes later he's sticking his head in my room. "Corn Pops?"

I smile and get dressed fast and head into the

kitchen, where he's setting out bowls and spoons. "I hear someone got Mom to agree to a four-day backpacking trip?" he says.

We do a spoons-cheers and start in on our cereal, and I tell him all about the trip. How we're going to stay in tents and cook dinner on a tiny little burner, and how I'm excited to go on an adventure with Oliver but if I see a snake I'll croak, and how you have to carry this water-bladder-holder thing that goes in your pack so you can drink and also have your hands free.

"Huh," Dad says. "Why do you need your hands free?" My dad is obviously not sporty like Oliver or Uncle Toby either.

But I guess I haven't really thought about why you'd need your hands free, because I can't think of a good reason either. "You know," I say. "In case I have an opportunity to catch dinner with my bare hands." Then I pretend I'm grabbing a fish from right out of a stream.

Dad laughs, and his laugh is the best, like giggly bubbles that spill out and multiply, and I'm the best at getting it.

He takes a big sip of orange juice, and I ask him about Rosalie. He's not allowed to tell me his patients' real names, so we give them fake ones when we talk about his work. Rosalie is eighty-two and her liver is sick.

Dad crunches a bite. "Comfortable at least, but

she's not going to get better."

"I know," I say, and look down at my Corn Pops. If I'm not allowed to know their real names, I'm pretty sure I'm not supposed to have a favorite, but Rosalie's my favorite. She's been in and out of Dad's care in the hospital for over a year, and she's full of what Dad calls spunk and fight. She's the only one who can get the doctors to laugh, and she makes every patient around her feel like family. But from the way Dad's talking, I don't think she'll be leaving the hospital this time.

"But enough about dear, fierce Rosalie," Dad says. "How's school?"

I say everything is great because it is, except I don't mention Reuben at all, and I figure I'll tell him all about how Oliver and I are creating a graphic novel superhero named Gabiver another time. I could eat a hundred bowls of Corn Pops, but Dad needs his rest, because he's kind of a real-life hero, one who helps sore and aching people be more comfortable.

Dad reaches across the counter and pats my hand with his. "Have a great day at school."

I love starting my day like this, with Dad's hero-hand touching mine, hoping some of it'll rub off on me.

I lean my bike in the rack outside school and reach for my phone to text Mom that I'm safe. Oliver's always here before I am, and I always lean my bike in next to his every morning. But he's not here yet. I look up to see if he's riding down the sidewalk, but he's not, and when I look back down, Reuben is parking his bike next to mine.

"Hi," I say.

He smiles and gives me a quick wave while he adjusts his handlebars so they're straight. I don't know what else to say, so I adjust mine, too, and then we start toward the school. We're not walking together, but we're not *not* walking together, and I'm wondering if it looks like we're really-actually walking together, like friends do. And I'm kind of hoping it doesn't, and that feels rotten, but it also feels weird not talking, so I say, "Hope you like our school."

Reuben shrugs like he's saying *It's fine*, and holds the door open for me.

Chaz is in the lobby with a circle around him, saying the whole bet should have been called off, that it wasn't fair, because Ms. Leavitt wasn't even trying to get the new kid to talk.

I can feel my face turning a little red, and Reuben's does, too, and I can't think of anything to say, so I just kind of blurt out, "I like your bike." Reuben nods, and then I pretend to look around for Oliver, even though I know he's not here.

I'm walking away from Reuben through the groups of sixth, seventh, and eighth graders when Oliver finally arrives.

"Where were you?" I ask.

He tightens the straps on his book bag. "My mom called a family meeting this morning." He rolls his eyes and says it was about nothing, and then morning bell rings, and we head toward Ms. Leavitt's room together.

She gives us fist bumps on the way in, and we sit at our tables, and she sets the timer for *Moment of Meditation*. I take out my mom's list of backpacking stuff, and Oliver and I scooch together to look.

"I have all those things already," he whispers.

"Hey, why do we need a fancy water-bladder-holder thing anyway?" I ask.

He doodles a picture of a plastic bag–type thing, connected to a long hose and mouthpiece. "Water comes from here, and you suck it through here," he says, pointing. "That way you can keep your hands free for a rock scramble or to grab a skinny tree and pull yourself to summit."

"Rock scramble?" I say.

Oliver laughs and says, "Like when the trail gets steep and rocky and you need to use your hands to get up. You have to be ready for anything."

I turn Oliver's drawing of the fancy water-bladder-holder thing into a character by adding eyes, a mouth, and legs. The hose is its nose. Then I sketch a speech bubble coming up and write, *Look! No hands!* Oliver and I hide little laughs in the crooks of our elbows, and Ms. Leavitt comes over to check it out and laughs with us too.

Then she tells us all to find a good stopping place for our *Moment of Meditation* and to take out our folders so we can get right to work on our projects. She's giving us class time every day until it's due to work on it, but I know Ms. Leavitt. If we're not using the time well, she'll take it right back.

I'm pulling out our sketches of Gabiver from yesterday when the classroom door opens.

Principal Tacker walks in, and all the kids who are talking, even if they're talking about their projects, immediately shut their mouths and pretend they're busy at work.

Then the girl from the office walks in behind her. She has on a different bandanna than yesterday, but her short, light brown hair sticks up the same way all around it, and her face still looks hard and annoyed.

"This is Rae," Principal Tacker says. "She's a seventh grader, but she'll be joining your class for as long as it takes her to write an apology letter that she's been reluctant to write." Rae rolls her eyes.

Ms. Leavitt's face seems a little surprised, but she quickly covers it with a smile and says, "Welcome, Rae. You can take a seat wherever you'd like." Then she asks Principal Tacker for a word in the hallway.

I can't hear what they're saying out there, especially because as soon as she closes the door everyone starts talking again.

Rae looks around the room, then walks toward Reuben's table and sits down in the seat right next to him.

Chaz snorts and leans over and whispers loudly, "Reuben doesn't talk. Like, ever. You might want to switch tables."

Jade snorts, and Missy and Tonya hide giggles behind their hands.

Rae shrugs and looks at Reuben. "You mind if I sit here?"

Everyone watches as Reuben shakes his head.

There are a few snickers in the classroom, then Chaz starts humming that *Rae and Reuben sittin' in a tree* song.

I'm trying hard not to laugh, but I'm picturing Reuben and Rae up in a tree K-I-S-S-I-N-G. Oliver chuckles a little, too, and that makes me feel like maybe it's OK to laugh at this one since Oliver's my best friend and I know he'd never do anything mean. So I do it. I let out a snicker, and for a second it feels good to be laughing along, like I might be earning some cool points too.

Then Rae whips her head around and stares right at Chaz, then Orin and Jade and Missy and Tonya and everyone else. Even me. "You all are a bunch of babies," she says, and I immediately feel it in my guts.

Ms. Leavitt comes back in and says we're so lucky to have another new student and we should all welcome Rae. "I'm sure she'll be a wonderful addition to our class."

Rae scoffs and says, "More like Principal Tacker doesn't know what to do with me."

Ms. Leavitt looks over the glasses on her nose and says, "Well, Principal Tacker's not here now, so that's enough about that," and she gives Rae that look that says *When you're in my room, you're my business.*

Then Ms. Leavitt just carries on like nothing is out of the ordinary. Like we don't have a troublemaking seventh grader sitting in our classroom right next to Reuben, who doesn't talk.

"Let's continue with the work for our projects," she says.

Some kids move to sit on the rug near the library, and others join with partners at different tables. I look at our Gabiver sketch and pull my chair a little closer to the table.

Then Oliver nudges me and points at Rae. She's leaning back in her chair with one knee against the table, talking to Reuben.

"Have you decided what you're doing for your project?" she asks him.

Reuben nods.

"I remember doing this last year in Ms. Garrison's class," she says. "I took all these old photographs of my grandma and made copies and kind of transformed them into self-portraits. It didn't have any words or anything."

Reuben raises his eyebrows.

"You're wondering how that tells a story," she says to him, like she can tell what he's thinking. "The pictures told the story of my family. We're a lot alike, my grandma and me," she says. "Ms. Garrison said it was beautiful and worth a thousand words."

Reuben smiles and nods.

"How can she just talk to him like that?" Oliver whispers. "Without him talking back." I shrug, but really I'm thinking it's actually not so hard. You just kind of do, you talk, and watch, and talk some more.

Rae taps two Sharpie pens against her knee like drumsticks. "So what are you doing for your project?"

Reuben stares at her for a couple of seconds and

ruffles some papers in his folder, but then Chaz looks over and whispers, "Rude Reuben who never replies."

And then Orin mumbles something under his breath, and Saunders laughs and so does Jolene, and then the giggles kind of spread to the next table because Ingrid is laughing now too.

"Hold on a minute," Rae says to Reuben. She stands up and gives Chaz another look, then sits back down next to Reuben and asks, "Are they always like this?" And I'm wondering if she means me too when she says *they.*

Reuben nods, and then he points to the blank piece of paper in front of her, the paper she's supposed to be writing on so she can get back to her seventh-grade class.

"I'm not actually going to apologize for what I did," she says.

He taps the paper and raises his eyebrows again in a question. Then she leans in and starts whispering to him. I try to block out all the other sounds in the room of people working on their projects and hear just her because I really want to know what she did to get sent out of her class and into ours. And it seems like I'm not the only one who wants to know because as soon as she starts whispering everyone gets quiet, and then quieter, and then kind of bends toward her. When she realizes that the room's silent, she looks up and laughs.

"Well, if everyone wants to know," she says, "I'll just say it out loud."

She looks at Ms. Leavitt, who gestures for her to go ahead.

"I'm supposed to apologize to my English teacher because I said a bad word," she tells us. "But it wasn't my fault, because for our next project we're writing reviews for our favorite book, but she said we can't choose graphic novels, because they don't count."

"What?" I say. And I don't mean to say it out loud, but I can't believe it. "What does she mean they don't count?"

Rae looks up and says in a loud, fake whisper across the room, "Don't worry; I'm not apologizing. *She* said it was a bad word, but I think it was appropriate for the situation."

"Then it seems you'll be in our room for the rest of the year," Ms. Leavitt says, but she doesn't say it like she's disappointed. She says it like maybe this room is right where Rae belongs.

Then Ms. Leavitt smiles and says, "OK, everyone, back to your projects."

Everyone starts talking again, and I hear whispers about *What word do you think she said?* I'm wondering that, too, and so is Oliver because he leans in and says,

"Do you think it was like starts-with-*d* bad or starts-with-*f* bad?"

I shrug, but then Rae's voice is right behind us. "It was starts-with-*h* bad," she says. "What're you making?"

"A comic," I tell her; then I measure out some more frames on the paper and move a little closer to Oliver.

"Looks like a good character," she says, pointing to our sketch of Gabiver.

"It's half me, half him," I say.

She smiles, pulls up a chair, and says, "Like Dog Man."

"Exactly!" Oliver says. "We're starting the story on the day we met in pre-K, and we're going to need emergency stitch-us-together surgery."

He starts sketching out the playground at our pre-K building while I tell him what characters to add in. "Ms. Carrie," I say. "And you and me on the teeter-totter."

This is actually one of my first memories. I remember my mom came ten minutes early for pickup. I saw her car pull in, and she watched us on the playground until another mom showed up. Then she got out and stood by the edge.

One by one kids left with their grown-ups, but I begged Mom to stay just a little longer because I had never been brave enough for a teeter-totter before, but that day Oliver was sitting on one side, his body all the way lowered to the ground. I remember thinking the curls of his hair looked like the long, twisty slide I was still too scared to go down.

Then he stood up from the teeter-totter, and the other side lowered to the ground. "Climb on," he said. "We can do it together."

And if you lined up a thousand kids, I wouldn't have gotten on a teeter-totter with 999 of them. But Oliver was number one thousand.

I fell off on my first try and came up with wood chips from the playground stuck all over my knees, but I didn't cry. "Get back on," Oliver said. "Try again." So I did. And I loved the way my belly flipped with every lift and fall.

Pretty soon it was just us two left, and Ms. Carrie told my mom she was welcome to take me home and she would wait with Oliver for his mom.

"Oh, that's OK," Mom said. "What's a teeter without a totter?"

We've been best friends ever since.

Rae's still watching us work, and she says it's a good beginning, but we need a crime or a mystery or something, as if we don't know that already.

She returns to her spot next to Reuben, and we

spend the whole period sketching our pre-K playground, and when the bell rings Ms. Leavitt says she'll see us tomorrow.

I watch Rae zip up her book bag. "What do we have now?" she asks Reuben. "Science?" He shakes his head. "Gym?" He shakes again.

I hear Chaz kind of snickering; then he says, "For a silent guy, he sure has a chatty girlfriend."

Rae whips around and says, "I'm getting the feeling *you* could benefit from a little more silence."

That shuts Chaz up pretty quickly. Then she turns back to Reuben. "Math?" she says. He nods.

"Great, see you there." Then she heads out the door ahead of him.

At the end of the day, Oliver says he's going to practice some free throws on the playground court, and I head to the office to give Ms. Phillips the forms so I can start Nature Club.

"I'll get these processed and let Mr. Jasper know to expect you Monday," she says. "They meet in the gazebo by the playing fields."

I nod *thanks*, and as I'm turning to go, Oliver's mom comes into the office. And before she even has time to notice me, and before I can even say hi, she's holding out her hand, palm up, toward Ms. Phillips.

"I'm here for Oliver Quick's cell phone. Somebody here took it from him yesterday."

"Let me get Principal Tacker for you," Ms. Phillips says.

Oliver's mom looks different. Her hair is longer maybe, or grayer, and I realize I haven't seen her in a long time. When we were younger we used to play at his house a lot, and his three sisters would set up obstacle courses that sent us flying down their basement stairs in cardboard boxes and read us fairy tales from their old picture books in forts that we built from couch cushions.

But then, at the beginning of fourth grade, his dad left and his mom started working more shifts at the restaurant in town, and last year Oliver's oldest sister, Layla, went to college, and now Shawna and Rebecca are in high school, and maybe we're too big for couch-cushion forts.

So Oliver started coming over to my house instead, and it just stuck. I can't even remember the last time I was over there, flying down their basement stairs.

Principal Tacker greets Oliver's mom and says, "I'm sure you've read the handbook, but we have a strict policy about cell phones in school." She's going on about distractions and screen time, and I realize I'm just standing there, all the way against the far wall of the office, staring at Oliver's mom, because it's not just her hair that's different. It's her skin, and her eyes, which are kind of watery and have dark, baggy moons underneath.

Principal Tacker hands over the cell phone, and Oliver's mom holds it up and shakes it between them. "I pay the bills for this phone," she says. "Not you."

Principal Tacker tries to respond, "I understand that, Ms.—"

But Oliver's mom just keeps on talking. "You don't have permission to take this from my kid. I can't be leaving work and coming down here to get my own *damn* phone."

I can feel my eyes bug out of my head because Oliver's mom said a starts-with-*d* bad word to Principal Tacker.

She turns fast to leave the office, and I look down and pretend to be busy putting something in my book bag so she doesn't see me. I zip my bag slowly and count to twenty before leaving so there's no chance of me running into her in the parking lot when I head out for my bike.

It's warm when I get outside, maybe even hot, and everyone is taking off their sweatshirts and pointing their faces to the sun, twirling and laughing on the sidewalk. I take my sweatshirt off, too, and stuff it in my book bag. Then I strap on my helmet and pedal fast toward the bookstore, and I say, "Damn," right out loud to the wind, and it feels kind of good and makes me laugh. But then I feel kind of weird because Oliver's mom isn't the kind of person to say *damn* in the principal's office. She didn't say *damn* when we knocked a lamp off the table at the end of our cardboard run down her basement stairs. Or when we dripped red Popsicle on one of her blankets that we draped over our living room fort. Or even when she told Oliver that his dad was moving to a tiny town called Troivo in Massachusetts, which Oliver and I had to look up on a map.

I think most moms would say *damn* in any one of those situations.

But Oliver's mom never did.

6.

TODAY I GET TO hang out at the bookstore for two whole hours after school because Mom has to work later than usual.

She's opening boxes of new arrivals in the back office, and when I poke my head in, she says, "Hey, have you heard of the timber rattlesnake?"

"Endangered, Mom."

She laughs and pulls me in for a hug and says I can unbox the next one, but then she has to work, so I get to read on the store's porch until she's done.

"Here," she says, pushing a box across the floor to me. "I saved this for you."

I rip the tape from the top, fold back the cardboard flaps, pull out the plastic bubble filling, and can't believe what's sitting inside. It's a whole box full of copies of *All Thirteen*, the book about the Thai boys' soccer team that got trapped in a cave and all the heroes who rescued them. I got it for Christmas and read the whole thing out loud with Oliver, every day of the whole school break, and it was better than TV.

I pick up a copy from the box and hold it to my chest.

"You already have it, Gabe," Mom says.

"But my copy doesn't have all the stickers on it," I say. The book won a zillion awards after we read it, and now the dust jacket is covered with shiny circles.

Mom laughs and says, "You really are my kid." Then she puts her hand out for the book. "And these are a special order for a school, so I need that back."

The store's phone starts to ring, so I hand the book back to Mom and she nods toward the door and says she'll check on me later.

There are two rocking chairs out on the wraparound porch. I pull one into the sun and watch groups of kids push their bikes up the street from school toward the library and the country store with sweatshirts under their arms. It's finally starting to feel like Spring. There are a couple of families with little kids gathering on the town green with blankets spread out and a few joggers in shorts and T-shirts bouncing on their toes waiting for the light to change.

I take out the new Dog Man, and with the sun on my skin, I start to read and I can feel myself fall right into the story. This is what happens when I'm reading a good book. I pretend I'm right there in the story, and I can see it all like it's a movie. It happened when Oliver and I were reading *All Thirteen*, and it's happening now because I don't even look up once until someone comes and stands right in my sun and sends a shadow across my page.

"Working on your tan?" Oliver says. He's still wearing his basketball clothes and sweating, but he pulls the other rocking chair up in the sun next to me.

I ask him how his free throws were and he says OK, and I'm about to tell him I saw his mom in the office, but then I decide not to because it feels weird that I didn't say hi to her, and it feels weird that she said *damn*.

Mom comes out right then and says, "Hey there," to Oliver and hands me some money. "It's warm," she says. "And it's Vermont, so you never know if it'll snow again tomorrow. You boys better get some creemees while the sun's out." It takes us zero seconds flat to hop up and cut across the green to the country store, leaving our chairs rocking behind us.

We lick our maple-chocolate twists on the way back to the bookstore and search the community bulletin board outside on the porch while we finish our cones.

There are help wanted ads, garage sale announcements, guitar lessons, tutoring services, and kids' summer camps. I see a new one, on bright green paper, stapled next to a notice about registering to vote. *Wanted: Mother's Helper. To play with my two-year-old twins while I work out in the basement. Flexible hours. $12/hr. Call Paula.* Oliver's looking at it, too, because his hand reaches up and rips off one of the tabs with the person's phone number.

"We could do this," he says.

"We?" I say. "Like, us?" I point to him, then back to me.

He nods. "Yeah, us."

"Babysitting?" I say. "No way. I can't even keep a hamster out of the road."

"Their mom is going to be home the whole time," Oliver says. "We just have to stack blocks and stuff."

"Why would we even *want* to stack blocks and stuff?" I ask.

"I don't know," he says. "It might be nice to make a little money." He looks down at the phone number in his hand. "You know, for the backpacking trip." Then he starts to talk really fast. "One of my hiking socks has a hole, and I want a wicking shirt so I don't have to hike in cotton."

"Why can't you hike in cotton?"

"You can," he says. "It just gets wet and stays wet, and the wicking ones pull the sweat away from your body and don't stink as much."

"That sounds like magic," I say.

Oliver laughs and takes a bite of his cone. Then he shrugs. "I think we should do it." He's rolling the ripped-off paper with the phone number on it between his sticky creemee–fingers.

"I can stack blocks," I say.

Oliver rides home with us and stays for dinner, and when I cut a bite of chicken I tell Mom about the mother's helper job we found on the community board.

"No," Mom says. "You aren't old enough to be babysitters. Believe me."

"It's not a babysitter; it's a mother's helper," Oliver says.

"Their mom is going to be home the whole time," I add.

Mom gives me a look that says *And I'm home the whole time you play with Puppy, and she still rolls into the street.* But two-year-olds don't just roll into streets. At least I'm pretty sure.

"Why do you even *want* to be mother's helpers?" she asks. "Neither one of you has younger siblings. I think you might be underestimating how hard it is, even just for a couple hours. Heck, a couple *minutes* can be hard."

I look at Oliver, thinking he'll back out. "I could use the money," he says. "For the backpacking trip."

I nod with him and say, "Plus, together we can do anything! Because together we're . . . Gabiver!"

Mom laughs, and I tell her that maybe we could do it Tuesday and Thursday after school and then she can work later at the store even on the days I don't have Nature Club. She raises her eyebrows, and we both know this is a good argument.

"Mom," I say. "This is how I learn responsibility."

She takes a deep breath and exhales. "Fine," she says. "You can call after dinner to get more information."

Oliver smiles and takes a bite of chicken, and after dinner we unfold the phone number from the flyer and run upstairs to my bedroom to make the call.

Puppy is spinning on her squeaky exercise wheel, so I throw in a couple of pieces of the chopped carrot from her treat container to keep her quiet. She tumbles out of her wheel and grabs a piece with both tiny paws and begins nibbling.

Oliver and I do rock, paper, scissors best two out of three, and I lose, so I'm the one who has to call.

I dial the number, and just when I think it's going to go to voice mail a woman answers.

"Hi," I say. "My name is Gabe Mackey, and I saw

your flyer at the country store."

She sounds nice, but I also think she might be holding the phone squished between her shoulder and her ear like my mom sometimes does at the bookstore when she's using both hands to skim through a shelf, checking to see if they have a copy for a customer.

I tell the woman about Oliver. "There will be two of us," I say. And I have to actually bite my tongue to stop myself from saying, *Together we're Gabiver!*

"Oh, wonderful," she says. "If it works out, maybe I could bump up the rate to sixteen dollars per hour so it's a more worthwhile split."

"That would be great!" I say, and I give Oliver a thumbs-up.

Then I hear Mom in my doorway. I turn around and try to wave her off like *I can do this.* But she's whispering, "Ask her questions. Like, what hours is she looking for? What are the kids' names? Are they potty-trained?" She gestures circles with her hand like I should have a hundred more questions after those ones.

"What are the kids' names?" I ask.

"Knox and Kobe."

"And do they . . . you know, go on the potty?"

"Ha! No, not yet," she answers. "Have you ever changed a diaper?"

"Yeah!" I say. But really, no.

"Oh, wonderful," she says. "You must have younger siblings?"

"N-no, I just . . . practiced on dolls."

There's a huge crash like she just dropped a pot in the kitchen. Or a bunch of pots. "Shoot, hold on," she says. Then it sounds all staticky-under-watery. Then another crash. "Do you think you could come this weekend to meet the boys? Saturday at three fifteen?"

I whisper to Oliver and he nods.

"Sure," I say, and write down the address she gives me. Then there's another loud crash and crying, and she hangs up.

I look at Mom. "You practiced *what* on dolls?" she asks.

My cheeks turn hot.

"Gabe, did you just tell that woman you practiced diapering on dolls?"

"Maybe?"

She rolls her eyes, then comes in my room and checks out the address I have scribbled on my notebook. "Well," she says, throwing one arm around me and one around Oliver. "At least it got you boys an interview."

7.

THE NEXT DAY IN Ms. Leavitt's class, Oliver has his cell phone back and he's sneaking it in his lap beneath our table, looking down, then jotting things in his notebook during *Moment of Meditation*. I try to look at what he's doing but can't see.

I want to tell him that he probably doesn't ever have to hide his phone anymore, because after his mom came in and told everyone in the office whose *damn* phone that is, I don't think even Principal Tacker would dare take it.

"I'm just checking the NBA scores," he whispers when he notices me looking. "My TV broke."

I shrug and say, "Sorry." But really, I don't even know what teams are playing. My parents never really watch sports, neither do Oliver's mom and sisters, but his dad is originally from Ohio and a big LeBron James fan, and he never missed a game.

When we were little, Oliver's parents argued, and sometimes they yelled, but I remember the day his dad left in fourth grade because when my mom told me about it that night, I didn't understand that a person could just leave and be gone, and it made me sad. The next day in school I pressed my shoulder even tighter into Oliver's, and he told me that his dad had folded a LeBron jersey and left it on his bed for him. He was wearing it that next day, and then the next, and the next, even when Chaz started teasing him for never taking it off. The jersey's too small for him now, but that was the year Oliver started watching basketball. And playing.

While Oliver concentrates on his phone, I open my notebook and write one of those poems where you spell a word down the side of your paper. I don't even know why I do it. I can't remember the last time I wrote any type of poem, but my pencil just starts moving and before I know it, I think I've got a pretty good one.

Definitely not
Interested in
Any
Poop
Exiting two-year-old butts,
Really.

I nudge Oliver and slide my notebook over to him. He laughs and says, "That's your job."

"Not it!" we say at the same time. Then, "Jinx!"

Oliver pretends to sniff poop and plugs his nose, and we get into one of those giggle attacks where we just can't stop at all, and the harder we try, the more impossible it is.

And even though it's the good-down-in-your-guts kind of laughing, Ms. Leavitt tries to get us to quit it. "Gentlemen," she says.

It makes us both stop right away, but then out of the corner of my eye I see Oliver's shoulders start shaking, and before I can help it, my shoulders start going too. I try to think of something boring and terrible and sad. But all I can imagine is Oliver changing poopy diapers, so I spurt out another laugh. Then Oliver does too. And then we're giggling all over again.

"Go ahead. Get it all out," Ms. Leavitt says. "It's only going to get worse if you hold it in."

I look at Oliver and he looks at me, and I know what he's thinking because I'm thinking the same thing. *Get it all out? Hold it in?* He's laughing so hard now that his face is turning red, and I can feel mine heating up too.

Ms. Leavitt points to the door and says, "Rejoin us when you can control yourselves."

Control ourselves? Now we're laughing so hard that we're swallowing the laughs with each breath and just can't stop. It's the kind of laughing that hurts your belly and makes you cry, and it's definitely contagious because some of the other kids in class start laughing, too, even though they have no idea what's so funny.

Oliver closes his notebook and zips it in his book bag with his cell phone, and we hobble to the hall holding our bellies.

We can't stop when we get to the hall either. We try deep breaths and looking in opposite directions, but we just can't, and Oliver is crying so hard that it actually for a second looks like real tears, not giggle-attack tears, because he's gasping and sniffing and his chest is heaving and his laughs are slowing. But it isn't until Principal Tacker rounds the corner of the sixth-grade wing that our laughs quit completely in the back of our throats.

"Mr. Mackey. Mr. Quick. Can you tell me why you're *outside* of your classroom?"

"I . . . we . . ."

Then the door opens and Ms. Leavitt's there saying, "Thank you, Gabe and Oliver, for volunteering to be *it* first. We're ready for you now." Then she pretends to see Principal Tacker for the first time. "Oh, hello, Principal

Tacker. We're just doing a little community-building activity."

"Community building?" Principal Tacker says, raising her eyebrows. "It's April."

"It *is* April," Ms. Leavitt says. "And we just got two new members in our community. So, yes, building and rebuilding, because community is such an essential part of learning."

Our eyes go back and forth between the two like we're watching Ping-Pong, but Principal Tacker can't make a return, so Ms. Leavitt ends the match and puts her hands on our shoulders in a way that says *When you're in my classroom, even if you're laughing yourselves silly, you're my business.*

"Come on," she says, and nods for us to go through the door.

When we're back inside we nod thanks and return to our seats, and I quickly close my notebook because it's still open to the *DIAPER* poem, and I don't want to get started up all over again.

Most everyone is working on their projects, but when I glance back at Reuben, I accidentally catch his eye and then he cracks a smile and I do too. And then he lets out a laugh, and his shoulders start going, and I can feel that good laugh rising right back up through me, too, and we both giggle a little, trying to hide our laughs with the sleeves of our sweatshirts.

And when Chaz leans toward Saunders and says, "So he can hiccup *and* laugh," I pretend I don't hear and turn back to my table to work with Oliver on our comic.

At the end of the day Rae packs up her stuff and turns to Reuben in the hall.

"Bye," she says. "Have a good weekend."

Chaz ducks behind Reuben's back in the hallway and pretends to be his voice. He makes it all high-pitched and flowery. "Bye, Rae." And makes a big smooching sound. Reuben spins around, but Chaz is already standing back up, holding out his arms like *What? It wasn't me.* Orin and Saunders laugh and point at each other like it wasn't them either.

Reuben narrows his eyes and stares right at Chaz. At first Chaz tries to look right back at him, but he doesn't last more than five seconds in that staring contest, because Reuben's using a glare that would make Ms. Leavitt look away.

"Whatever, man," Chaz says, breaking his gaze and looking down at his sneakers. "You going to say anything or not?"

Rae throws her book bag over one shoulder. "Doesn't

seem like he needs to," she says. "He was clearly telling you not to try that guano again."

Orin and Saunders look at Chaz like *What the heck does* guano *mean?* and Chaz shrugs even though he's supposed to be a genius.

Rae rolls her eyes. "Get a dictionary," she says.

Then she heads down the hall as soon as the final bell rings. I can tell she's checking her cell phone on the way out because her head is bent down, and right in that moment Principal Tacker steps out of her office.

"Ms. Hendriks!"

Rae slides the phone in her pocket and keeps rushing right on by like she doesn't even hear her.

But Principal Tacker definitely sees the phone and says, "Hand it over," and holds out her palm.

"The bell already rang," Rae says. "The school day is over."

Principal Tacker still has her hand out for the phone. "You're still on school grounds, Ms. Hendriks. Rules are rules."

But Rae keeps right on walking. "It's not a good rule, though," she calls over her shoulder. "Have a good afternoon!"

Kids in the hallway are saying *Ooooo* as Principal Tacker walks back in her office, and if I had a thought

71

bubble above my head right now it'd be all exclamation points.

"Get Rae Hendriks's mom on the phone," Principal Tacker says.

We're all looking through the glass windows of the office, hoping to hear what she says to Rae's mom, but Principal Tacker turns her back and we can't make out a thing.

Chaz laughs and mumbles, "Why isn't Rude Reuben sticking up for his girlfriend?"

Oliver hides a little snicker behind his hand, and even though it wasn't me laughing, I still feel gobbledy-gooky. Reuben shakes his head, and I can see he's clenching his teeth hard because little muscles bulge out from his jaw.

Principal Tacker pokes her head back out of the office and says, "Mr. Gilbertson!"

Finally, I'm thinking. But instead of busting Chaz for being mean to Reuben, she says, "I got an email about an essay contest through the high school that you might be interested in." She waves him into the office. "Your mom wanted me to give you a copy of the submission guidelines."

Orin nudges him and says, "Yeah, go on, Gifted Gilbertson."

Saunders laughs and fakes a cough into his elbow and says, "Nerd."

"Shut up," Chaz says, and pretends to laugh along with them. Then he nudges them back, and he walks to the office.

Oliver gestures to me and turns toward his locker. He pretends he's rummaging through his Sports Club bag, but I can see the glow of his cell phone screen. He nods for me to come closer, so I kind of stick my head in his locker as much as I can to read his screen: *guano [gwah-noh]: the excrement of seabirds and bats. Manure, muck, feces, waste.*

The giggle attack starts all over again, and I can already feel the sore muscles in my stomach from laughing so hard earlier. Tears squeeze from Oliver's eyes as he zips his phone back in his bag.

"Sports Club," he can barely say through his laughing. "See you tomorrow." The locker room doors close, and I head out to get my bike.

When I get outside I look over to the playing fields where most of the clubs meet. The basketball court is full of Sports Club kids already, stretching and hopping and warming up, and I see Mr. Jasper in the gazebo getting ready for Nature Club. I wonder if he knows yet that I'm starting on Monday, and I'm wondering what kinds of things you even do in a Nature Club. Catch butter-flies? Make wishes on dandelion puffs? The description on the flyer said . . . *learning to navigate our natural world.* We'll probably be making flower chains and collecting berries, and I don't know how that's going to help me backpack on the Appalachian Trail this summer, but all I have to do is not quit.

8.

REUBEN

THERE'S ANOTHER KID IN my class who feels my kind of sadness. I can hear it.

9.

MOM INSISTS ON COMING with us when we go meet Knox and Kobe. And when we pull into their driveway, she doesn't wait in the car; she follows us right up to the door to meet their mom, and I'm not even annoyed because now that we're here I'm realizing I'm not even sure what you say to two-year-olds.

Their house is big. It's not a mansion with a fountain and a flagpole or anything, but it has a porch that wraps all the way around the sides, and two different front doors we could knock on, and three spaces for cars in their garage. One part of the garage is piled with broken-down boxes, and there's a mini van parked in the other.

A tall woman wearing stretchy workout clothes and

her hair pulled into a bun on top of her head answers the door. "Hi, you must be . . ."

"Gabe," I say. "And this is Oliver." Then I gesture to my mom, who is standing over my right shoulder. "And that's my mom."

"Oh, hi," she says to my mom. "I'm Paula."

"Addie," my mom says. "But don't mind me."

Paula opens the door wide to welcome us in. She shows us to the kitchen, where the twins are in these little chairs that attach right to the counter. One is trying to use a spoon, but his hand is around the wrong end and he has yogurt smeared up to his elbow. The other is not even trying. He's going right into it with his fingers and getting some to his mouth while most slops into the pocket of a plastic purple bib. *Gross*, I'm thinking.

"Guys, can you say hi to Gabe and Oliver?"

"Hiiiiii!" they say, then make slurping sounds.

"This is Knox," she says, pointing to upside-down-spooner. "And Kobe." They both have light brown curly hair and green eyes and chubby cheeks.

My first thought is, *How do you tell them apart?* They're even wearing the same clothes. I'm trying to memorize *Knox-yogurt-elbow*. But then Paula lifts him out of the little chair thing and carries him to the sink. He stands on a tall stool, and she rinses the yogurt off his face and hands all the way up to his elbow, and by the time she's rinsing off the other kid, I forget which is which again.

"I'm just looking for two hours a couple days a week. Enough to work out in the basement or prepare dinner without any obstacles," Paula tells us. "Basically, a break." She and Mom laugh a little. Then she plants a kiss on one of the kids' cheeks while the other wraps around her leg. "Maybe from three thirty to five thirty or so?"

Oliver says, "We have clubs on Monday, Wednesday, Friday, but we could do Tuesdays and Thursdays."

"And maybe some weekends?" she asks.

Oliver looks at me, and I look at Mom, and we all nod.

Mom nudges me, which means *Ask more questions.*

I can't think of any, but it's quiet and everyone's looking at me, so I blurt, "How do you tell them apart?"

Everyone laughs, and Oliver says, "I was wondering the same thing!"

"I can just tell," Paula says. "But until you get to know them, here's a little trick." She puts the kid who's in her arms down and bends to the one that's around her leg. "Let me see your finger," she says. He raises up his left pointer finger, and she shows us a little brown freckle tucked in the crease behind his knuckle. "This is Kobe."

I smile, and Kobe unwraps from his mom's leg and shows off his freckle. "Knox not have one," he says.

Knox starts crying at this, but his mom bends down and picks up a stuffed bunny from the floor and says, "Here, can you see if Bunny's ear is OK?"

Knox sucks up his tears and says, "Bunny, bunny," and looks beneath the droopy ear of the stuffed animal. "He OK," he tells his mom, and just like that he forgets he was even crying.

Paula locks a baby gate across the bottom of the stairs and shows us around the first floor of their house.

There's a separate dining room with tall standing cabinets holding fancy-looking dishes and wineglasses. "Don't let them in here," she says, closing the double doors. "I just unpacked all that, and I don't need it to come crashing down."

She closes the big glass doors to their office, too, which has two flat-screen computer monitors, swively chairs, and a stack of moving boxes in the corner.

"New to the area?" my mom asks.

"Not new to Vermont," she says. "But new to town, yes."

Mom says, "Welcome," and then Paula shows us through the mudroom, and where the bathroom is, and the living room with an L-shaped couch and a fireplace, and a room she calls a sunroom, and their playroom, with a TV mounted on the wall, a basket overflowing with stuffed animals, shelves full of picture books and puzzles, and a chest of toys.

"No TV," she says. "But they love books, and Play-Doh, and anything with wheels, and . . . what else do you guys love?"

One jumps up and says, "Bunnies!" and the other says, "Cheese!"

"Got it," Oliver says, and gives them high fives. "We're going to have fun, aren't we?"

"Funnnnnn!" they say, and spin in circles and fall down.

When Paula shows us a drawer in the kitchen full of diapers and wet wipes, I try so hard not to laugh, but now I'm thinking about guano again, and I can tell Oliver is, too, and that makes it even harder.

"You probably won't even need these," she tells us, holding up a diaper. "But they're here, in case."

I say, "OK," and bite my tongue and try to change the subject fast. "Do they like playing outside?"

"Oh, of course!" Paula says. "We have a sandbox in the back, and a fleet of toy push lawn mowers, and bubbles and chalk in the garage, and whatever else you can find in there. They know they're supposed to stay in the yard, but they haven't exactly mastered the *Stop at the curb* rule yet. And they're fast, so you have to watch them."

My mom nudges me again. "See?" she whispers. But I roll my eyes because there's a difference between a four-ounce hamster and a couple of two-year-old human kids.

"So," Paula says. "What do you say? Do you think you could start right now?"

"Right now?" Oliver, my mom, and I all say.

"I'd love to get a workout in since you're here. We agreed on sixteen dollars an hour; is that right?"

I nod.

She looks at the clock. "It's three thirty now. Do you have a couple hours?"

Oliver says, "Yeah!" right away. I look at my mom because I don't actually know how to change diapers and what if . . .

But she just looks back at me like I shouldn't have lied, and I'd better hope they don't have to poop. "I'll pick you up at five thirty," Mom says. Then she leaves.

I look into the playroom, and Knox and Kobe are playing with blocks on the floor. I'm thinking this won't be so hard. We can stack blocks.

"OK," Paula says. "I'll be in the basement if you need anything." Then she pops in some earbuds, opens the basement door, and hustles down the stairs.

"This house is huge," Oliver whispers. "They have so many extra rooms they have to block them off." He points through the kitchen. "Have you ever heard of a sunroom before? I mean, what do you even do in there? Sit on that fancy padded bench and talk about the sun?"

Then he walks over and peeks through the double doors to their office. "Think she'd notice if I just take this room?"

I laugh, imagining Oliver walking down the street with their office on his back.

"I'd find a little piece of land in the woods and make it our own little house," he says. "I think it's big enough to fit my mom, my sisters, and me."

I'm about to say, "That room is not as big as your house," but I can't even answer him, because as soon as the sound of a treadmill starts downstairs, one of the twins picks up a block and tosses it at the other one. It hits him lightly in the arm, and the kid screams, "Ow!"

Oliver sits next to the kid who got hit, and I go to the hitter and uncurl his left finger. No freckle. "Knox," I say. "No throwing toys."

Oliver says, "Are you OK, Kobe?" And I swear Kobe *was* OK until Oliver asked, but then his lip starts to quiver and now he's crying.

Then Knox starts crying, too, like the tears are contagious, and pretty soon they both have thick snot mustaches. I get some tissues from the bathroom and try to wipe their noses, but they push my hand away like they prefer the snot mustaches to be there, growing and dripping down their lips. I'm really hoping Paula can't hear them crying forty seconds into our new job, and I'm thanking my lucky stars for those earbuds and hoping she's listening to the loudest metal music at the highest volume. But they're still crying, and I would do anything to get them to stop.

I try that bunny-ear trick, but it doesn't work.

"Do you want to go outside?" I ask.

Crying.

"Read a book?" I pull *The Very Hungry Caterpillar* off the shelf.

Still crying.

Then one of the kids sucks up his snot mustache. I can't tell which he is anymore, because they moved when I was getting the tissues, but he cries, "Yoyipop!"

"What?" I ask.

"Yoyipop!" he cries again. "I want a yoyipop!"

Then he gets up and walks into the kitchen and starts pulling open a drawer near the oven. I look inside and see a bunch of pot holders and oven mitts and dish towels. But he keeps pointing. "In there! Yoyipop."

Then his lip starts quivering again, so I dig through the towels and find, way in the back, a bag of vitamin C lollipops. "Oh! Lollipops!" I say. "Are you allowed to have lollipops?"

They're both there now, peeking in the drawer and nodding their heads. "Yoyipop in there. Pyease?" Both kids have same *y*-sounding *l*s, and both their hands are stretched out, so I check a left pointer finger. Freckle. Kobe.

They're not crying. But it's also before dinner, and Paula didn't say we could give them any food.

Knox stomps his foot.

But she didn't say we couldn't, either, so I unwrap two lollipops. They pop them in their mouths and it's immediately quiet. I stuff the wrappers in my pocket.

"OK, now let's read a book."

I go sit on the rug in the playroom and Oliver does too. The twins walk over and sit between us, and I turn to the first page of *The Very Hungry Caterpillar* and point to the little egg on the leaf. Then I'm thinking, *OK, this I can do. I can read for the next hour and fifty-two minutes*. But when we get to the part in the book where it's Saturday and the caterpillar is munching everything, one of the things it eats is a lollipop.

"Yoyipop," Knox says. Then he pulls the stick from his mouth, and he's bitten the whole thing off. "I'm done." He does a little gesture with his hands. "Another yoyipop, pyease."

"Me too!" says Kobe.

"Oh, no more lollipops today," I say. "But let's see what happens on the next page of the book."

Oliver takes the soggy stick from Knox and searches the kitchen for the garbage. He finds the right cabinet, but as soon as he drops the stick in, Knox chases him around the corner and screams, "No! That's my yoyipop! I want it back!"

"It was the stick. You were done. It's just garbage now. Yucky," Oliver tells him.

But it's too late. Knox is crying again, and then Kobe starts because he finished his lollipop, too, and the tears are definitely contagious.

I try to pull them back in to the book, but they aren't listening and before I can think of another thing to do, they start running. That's when I realize that the part of the first floor of their house that isn't blocked off is a big circle, because they fly past the mudroom, through the kitchen, past the sunroom table, through the living room, bouncing along the L-shaped couch as they go, and back into the playroom. Then through the kitchen again . . . One is chasing the other until he changes directions, and the chase starts all over again the opposite way.

"Aaaaaaaah!"

I'm standing in front of the dining room door,

making sure they don't burst through to the cabinets full of glass, and Oliver is standing in front of the office door, protecting the computer equipment.

He looks at me like *What do we do?* But I'm looking at him like that, too, so the next time they whip through the kitchen and past the office, Oliver puts his arms out and scoops one of them up in the air. The twin giggles and giggles, and the other one stops in front of me and wants a turn. I look at his finger.

"Kobe," I say. "You can have a turn, but then we're going to read another book. Deal?"

"OK," he says.

I put my hands beneath his arms and lift him as high as I can. It feels weird lifting a kid like this. He's heavier than I expected, and my arms start to shake after a few seconds of him pretending to be an airplane.

Then he points to Oliver and says, "I want a turn with Oyiver."

"Smart kid," Oliver says. "I give longer turns."

I roll my eyes and Kobe runs to Oliver, so Knox runs to me for a turn. I lift him as high as I can, which is already not as high as I lifted his brother the second before. Then the boys switch and I have Kobe again. They switch and switch and squeal with delight until my arms can't lift anymore. I look at my watch, thinking we probably have about an hour left. But it's only three forty-three. Mom left thirteen minutes ago. We have an hour and forty-seven minutes left.

And I really don't think I can do it.

But then I watch Oliver lift Kobe for one last airplane, and I'm thinking, we're Gabiver. We can at least get through the next one hour and forty-seven minutes, and then never come back again if we don't want to.

I look around for Knox. He's quietly touching the spines of the pictures books and making funny little grunting sounds, and I'm thinking, *Finally. We can just sit down and read some books.* But then Kobe looks over at Knox and says, "Knox go poopy."

I rush to him fast because I'm thinking maybe if I get to him in time I can hold him over the potty or something, and then we won't have a dirty diaper to change, and maybe Paula would give us a raise on the first day for potty-training her kid. But I know I'm too late when I get to him because I can smell it.

Oliver and I look at each other and say, "Not it."

Then Knox grunts one last time and starts running the circle of their house again. Past the mudroom, through the kitchen, by the table, through the living room, where he bounces across the L-shaped couch. "No, don't land on your—"

But it's too late. He landed on his butt. "I am *so* not changing that diaper," I say.

Then he runs back through the playroom, and Oliver catches him on the next loop.

"Should we just ask his mom?" Oliver says.

"We can't," I say. "I told her I knew how to do this."

I ask Knox to lie down on the floor and he says, "Yoyipop!"

"No, no. No more lollipops," I tell him, and he sits up fast and takes off for another loop around the circle.

Oliver gets a diaper and the package of wet wipes from the kitchen drawer and catches Knox again on his next loop through the playroom. Kobe is following him now and squealing, "Poopy! Poopy!"

"You have to get a clean diaper," Oliver says. "Come on, Knox."

"Yoyipop!"

We're Gabiver, I tell myself. So I try the bunny again. "Do you want to whisper a secret to Bunny?" I ask. He reaches out his arms and takes his bunny and starts whispering in his ear.

"I have yots of secrets," he whispers.

"Good!" I say. Kobe settles down next to me, and I wiggle Bunny in Knox's face a little while Oliver is wiping and wiping. He's using like a thousand wipes.

"I don't want to get it on my hands," he says.

Then Knox whispers into the bunny's ear, "I want a . . . YOYIPOP!"

"Me too!" yells Kobe, and he runs to the lollipop drawer in the kitchen and opens it and closes it and opens it and closes it again.

Oliver puts a hand on Knox's chest so he doesn't try to run his naked, poopy butt around the circle. "Just give him one!" Oliver calls. So I unwrap two lollipops from the drawer and stick them in their mouths, and just like that, it's quiet again.

"Find a bag or something," Oliver says. I open a few more drawers and find a bag of chips that's almost empty, so I pour the crumbs in my mouth and pass the bag to Oliver. He puts the dirty diaper in it and hands it back to me. I tie it up with a tight knot, and fast, because it stinks. Then I toss it outside on the step of their garage.

It takes us the entire lollipop to figure out that there are little built-in pieces of tape stuck to the diaper that fasten to the sides, and I think we might have put it on backward, but his butt is clean and covered and his pants are back up.

"Shoot," Oliver says. "We didn't put these in the bag." There's a mountain of wipes on the floor, and they smell too.

"I think we can flush those," I say. "They're like toilet paper, right?"

So we try.

But instead of the water in the bowl swirling down,

down, down it's now rising up, up, up. Oliver acts fast and grabs the plunger next to the toilet and gives three big thrusts until the water swirls all those wipes down and out of the bowl, but I'm pretty sure we clogged up their whole system. Neither one of us is brave enough to try flushing it again.

After a thousand more circle-runs around the house, we take them outside and chase them from the sandbox to the curb in the front yard, where they think it's a funny game to pretend they're going to run right out toward the street. Each time we catch them, they giggle and run again and again. "Chase me!"

I'm sweating and my arms are aching, and I'm certain that I'm not cut out to be a mother's helper. I'm ready to tell Paula that we gave it a try but two-year-old twins are harder than we thought, and she's going to have to find someone else.

At five twenty-five we bring the twins back inside and Paula's in the kitchen chopping vegetables. I think it still kind of smells like poop in here, and I'm wondering if she has some sort of mom-sixth-sense that Knox's diaper might be on backward and that we might have ruined her plumbing.

"How'd it go?" she asks. "I heard lots of laughter. That's a good sign!"

Oliver and I look at each other, and I'm wondering who's going to be the one who breaks it to her that we're not coming back. No way. But then she hands us two crisp twenty-dollar bills, and Oliver's eyes get as wide as basketballs.

"I don't have change," I tell her. "Maybe my mom . . ."

"Consider it a tip," she says. "You gave me some much-needed hours on short notice."

I look at Oliver again, and we each take a twenty from her hands, and Oliver says, "Thanks," and that we'll see her on Tuesday.

I look at him like *Are you kidding?* But he is not kidding, and if you lined up a thousand kids, you couldn't pay me to babysit again with 999 of them, but Oliver is number one thousand.

"Wonderful," Paula says, and bends down to kiss the tops of Knox's and Kobe's heads.

"And there's a dirty diaper tied in a chip bag on the garage step," Oliver says.

"Even more reason for a tip." Paula gives us a thumbs-up and says, "Thank you again," and we head out the door.

Mom is parked in the driveway when we get outside, and I limp toward her car like we just got beat up in a two-hour boxing match.

When we get far enough from the front door, Oliver whispers, "Of course we got stuck with guano!" Our giggle attack rises back up, and I can feel my sore stomach muscles.

Mom rolls down the window. "Get in, Oliver! We'll give you a ride home."

"Oh no, that's OK," he says. "I need to stretch my legs anyway. I'll walk."

I look at him funny because his house is all the way at the edge of town, and we've been doing nothing but running around and stretching our legs and arms and brains and everything all the way down to our pinkie toes for the past two hours, and I don't think I've ever been so tired.

But he says, "See you," and takes off down the street anyway, and I'm thinking that's about the sportiest kid who ever existed.

Before we pull out of the driveway, their front door opens and Knox and Kobe run out on the porch and lean over the railing to wave goodbye. Paula stands behind them with a spatula in her hand.

"Bye, Gabe!" they holler. "We yike you! We yike Oyiver!" And they're so cute with their wild hair and chubby cheeks that I almost forget about the crying and the running circles and the diaper fiasco. Almost.

And as they go back inside I catch something moving

in the upstairs window above the front door. It's a face. A person. And I know that face. I know that person.

It's Reuben.

The whole time Mom is cooking dinner she's asking me a hundred questions about how it went with the twins, but all I can think about is Reuben in the upstairs window. I'm wondering if I should send Oliver a message to see if he saw what I think I saw, but I know he was already halfway down the street when I looked up to that window. It can wait until Monday.

"Did they behave OK?" Mom asks. "What'd you do? Did you read them any books? Can you tell them apart now, or do you still need to look for the freckle?"

She's chopping garlic fast and asking me questions faster. "Did they beg for TV?"

But I have my own questions running through my head: *What was Reuben doing there? Did he see me? Is he Knox and Kobe's brother? And if he is, why isn't he his own mother's helper, and why can't he change his own brother's stinky diaper?*

"Gabe," Mom says, and snaps her fingers. "Was it fun?"

"Yeah," I say. "I mean, no. They threw stuff, and cried, and ran around in circles, and one of them pooped. I can't even remember which one now."

Mom laughs and slides the garlic off the cutting board into the saucepan. "Sounds about right," she says. "You think you'll stick with it?"

I nod and show her my twenty-dollar bill. "Oliver really wants to save up for some backpacking-trip stuff," I tell her. "And I'm not going to quit on him."

Mom smiles and puts her arm around me. "What a responsible thing to say." Then she opens a drawer, pulls out a black Sharpie marker, writes *Gabiver's Backpacking Collection* across the empty ziti box on the counter, and hands it over. I smile and drop the money in.

"Good start," she says. "That ought to get you at least one pair of fancy hiking socks."

Before I go to bed that night, I empty four crinkled lollipop wrappers from my pocket into the trash. Then I wonder again about Reuben and if that was really him in the upstairs window or if my mind was just playing tricks on me, because what would Reuben be doing up there?

The next day, Dad has off, and when those days fall on a weekend, we both sleep in and instead of Corn Pops, it's pancakes. I come downstairs when he's whisking batter and see Baby lying on my place mat. Baby is a ragged doll with a plastic face and eyes that flutter closed when you lay her down. I haven't seen Baby since our trip to

Scotland to visit Nana when I was six.

On our flight home we sat next to a pilot who was traveling to the United States for his next flight, and I had Baby tucked beneath my arm. The pilot explained what a cockpit looks like, and I imagined how it would feel to fly over clouds and clouds and sky and sky and ocean and ocean that spread as far as you could see. It made my stomach twist.

He handed me a sticker of airplane wings and said, "Now you can be a pilot too." And when I was about to thank him, the pilot tugged on Baby's foot. "But you'll have to get rid of her first. Big boys don't carry around dolls. Especially when they're flying 200,000 pounds of titanium, steel, and fuel across the Atlantic Ocean." Then he smiled up at my dad like he was doing him a favor.

I leaned over to stuff Baby in my carry-on bag, but Dad caught my arm and said, "Big boys don't tell others what they should and shouldn't do." So I held on to Baby, but near the armrest between Dad and me and as far from that pilot as I could.

I was sleeping when we got home from that trip, and Dad carried Baby and me up to my bed from the car. When I woke up the next morning, I wrapped Baby in her pink blanket, brought her down to the basement, and laid her on the storage boxes. I told my dad I didn't want to play with her anymore. He wrinkled up his forehead and frowned and said, "We'll keep her in the basement in case you need her again." I haven't seen her since.

Now Dad is standing in the kitchen with his apron on, whisking batter to the beat of his Sunday-morning playlist coming through the speaker. "Remember her?" he asks, nodding toward Baby.

"Yeah," I say, and I can immediately see that pilot's face in my mind. "But why—"

"I heard you might have told some woman that you knew how to change diapers because you practiced on dolls." A big smile spreads across his face. "So, get practicing."

While the pancakes cook on the griddle, Dad helps me fold dish towels around Baby's butt and fasten tape around her hips until I get it.

"It's a little harder when they're running around in circles," I say. "Baby doesn't do that."

Dad laughs and nods. "That's definitely true."

Mom joins us and inspects Baby's homemade diaper and gives me a high five. Then we eat pancakes and talk about Knox and Kobe and how hard it is to take care of little kids even for just two hours.

"That's why mothers need helpers," Mom says.

For some reason that gets us all laughing, and I'm so close to telling them about how I think I might have seen Reuben in the window upstairs. But I'm pretty sure that it couldn't have been him anyway. Plus, I haven't even told Mom and Dad about Reuben joining our class, and I don't know why except that I think they'd ask me if I want to have him over, or if I've been kind and welcomed him, and I don't have good answers for any of those questions yet.

10.

I TRY NOT TO look at Reuben in class on Monday, but I can't help it. We're working on our projects in Ms. Leavitt's class, and when Oliver bends over our paper to continue drawing the first scene for our *Gabiver* comic, I glance across the room to Reuben's table.

He's looking right back at me. And I swear I see one side of his mouth curl into a smile like he's saying, *I know you clogged our toilet* or *You had to bribe them with lollipops?*

I turn away fast and wait for Oliver to finish drawing the teeter-totter on the page. It looks exactly like the one from pre-K, with the same square, plastic seats right next to the sandbox. I've sketched out the whole scene, and Oliver is drawing the final version. Then I'll add the speech bubbles, how he invited me on and said *Try again* when I fell, and how my mom said, *What's a teeter without a totter?*

"Hey," I whisper, and I lean in toward Oliver. "You want to hear something weird?"

Oliver nods but keeps drawing.

"I think I saw Reuben in the upstairs window when we were leaving Knox and Kobe's house."

"What?" he whispers back. This time he looks up from the comic. Then he glances back at Reuben, who's sketching light pencil lines on a piece of notebook paper. Oliver turns back around and whispers, "Why would he be in their house?"

"I don't know," I say. "Maybe he's their brother?"

"Then why wouldn't *he* be babysitting?" Oliver asks. "I know for a fact if I had little brothers, my mom wouldn't be paying someone else to watch them. She'd be having me do it for free."

"That's what I was wondering," I say. "It couldn't have been him."

Talking about Reuben in whispers feels like gobble-dygook guts, and I'm thinking maybe I should just walk over and ask him. Say, *Hey, did I see you at Knox and Kobe's house on Saturday?* But no one talks to Reuben.

Except for Rae.

"Yeah, it was probably nothing," I say.

We're getting back to work on *Gabiver*, choosing colors for the scene, when the classroom door opens and Rae walks in. She hands a late pass from the office to Ms. Leavitt. "Principal Tacker's making me write two apology notes now," she says. "And I'm not sorry about this one either."

Ms. Leavitt slides the note on her clipboard. Then she smiles at Rae and points toward the door. But she doesn't point the way Principal Tacker points kids from the hallway into her office with her eyebrows all crumpled down, like she means business. Ms. Leavitt is pointing like she just wants to chat with Rae. Maybe she means business, too, but a different kind of business.

Rae sighs and follows Ms. Leavitt outside the classroom. "You all continue working," Ms. Leavitt calls, and she leaves the door open as she talks in a hushed voice with Rae.

It only takes Chaz a couple of seconds to say, kind of under his breath, "Rude Reuben's girlfriend is here."

Saunders and Orin laugh, and Reuben shoots them a look.

"What?" Chaz says. "Are you going to tell Ms. Leavitt on me? Oh, wait . . ."

Saunders and Orin laugh again, and Reuben bites down hard on his back teeth. I can see those two little knots bulge out from his jaw. He shakes his head and gets back to work on his sketch.

Oliver's laughing a little now, too, and since we're sitting shoulder to shoulder, I can feel the vibrations of his laugh in my body, and I wish he would stop because it feels rotten.

At recess Oliver joins in the basketball game, and I start sketching the big collision scene for our *Gabiver* comic. When I look up, I watch the game a little, and Jolene fakes right and goes left around Saunders on the basketball court.

I hear Missy squeal as she pumps high on the swing and flies off through the air, landing on her feet. Ingrid is chasing Lenny up a slide, and Fiona and Cass are racing across the monkey bars.

Then my eyes drift to Reuben. He's in the same spot. As far from the playground as possible, his body pressed against the red brick of the school building. He's watching everyone on the playground. I can see his eyes move from the concrete tunnel, where a couple of kids from Ms. Garrison's class are hiding, to the tall spiderweb structure, where five kids are climbing. He watches Tanya chase Andre across the bouncy bridge and flinches when a recess aide blows her whistle and tells them to walk. He watches Oliver dribble the ball hard into the pavement.

Then his eyes move toward Rae, who's sitting in

the gazebo peering into her book bag, with both hands shoved deep inside. She looks up and glances around every few seconds, then looks back in her book bag. And I know exactly what she's doing. She's on her cell phone. Probably texting her friends from seventh grade and definitely getting away with it.

Reuben can tell, too, because a smile spreads across his face. He watches her for a moment, then moves his eyes back to Oliver on the court. He's dribbling fancy moves around the other players and sends a hard bounce pass to Orin, who shoots and misses, but Oliver is there for the rebound.

Someone from the swing set calls, "Why don't you get some binoculars!" but Reuben doesn't seem to care, and he doesn't quit watching.

Oliver dribbles one last *Bam* into the pavement and jumps up for a shot, then fights again for the rebound but loses the ball. "God!" he yells, and pounds his fist into his thigh.

"Just a game," Saunders says, and tosses him the ball.

Oliver laughs him off, but the *Bam. Bam. Bam.* of his dribbling echoes off the bricks of the school wall behind Reuben.

11.

AT THE END OF the day Oliver closes his locker and says, "Good luck at Nature Club. Try to learn some stuff so you can survive on the trail." Then he laughs and says, "Like how to poop in the woods."

And we start all over with another giggle attack, except this time he has to go to the locker room to get changed for Sports Club, and my giggles fade out because I actually haven't thought about that yet. How *do* you poop in the woods?

I'm the first one to get to Nature Club. It's another sunny day, but the breeze makes me zip up my sweatshirt. Mr. Jasper, who is also the seventh-grade science teacher, is laying out three canvas daypacks on the gazebo bench.

"Hey," he says. "Gabe, right?"

I nod.

"I'm Mr. Jasper." He's tall and skinny and wears glasses on his face and a pair of binoculars around his neck.

I say it's nice to meet him, then I look around at the other clubs gathering in the schoolyard.

Oliver's running out from the locker room doors on the side of the school to the basketball courts. He gives fist bumps to a couple of seventh and eighth graders, then Corey and Lenny and Jolene from our class run out after him too. And then the whole court seems to be full of kids wearing athletic shorts and zip-up sweatshirts and chasing after the basketballs that Ms. Neely empties from her bag. The balls bounce and roll, and kids rush to them and start dribbling and doing all these quick, complicated-looking, through-the-leg fake-outs, then passing to each other and shooting.

"Did you try to get into Sports Club?" Mr. Jasper asks. I look up at him. "It's OK," he tells me. "I won't be offended."

Ms. Neely blows her whistle, and the kids gather in four lines across the courts. She blows her whistle again, and they drop down for five push-ups.

"That?" I say, pointing to the sweaty push-uppers on the court. "No."

Mr. Jasper laughs and says, "They basically begged me to facilitate Sports Club." Then he pretends to flex his very skinny arm muscles. "But I felt like it was the right thing to do to give Ms. Neely the chance."

Ms. Neely is now down on the court doing push-ups with all the kids, blowing her whistle for each one. Some kids drop to the pavement and moan, but Ms. Neely keeps on going until it's just one kid and her left.

"I guess she's doing OK," Mr. Jasper says, and I laugh.

Then Rae and another girl arrive at the gazebo, and they both grab daypacks and sling them over their shoulders.

"Vera. Rae," Mr. Jasper says, pointing to each of the girls. "Gabe." Then he points to me.

I kind of wave, and Rae says, "Oh, I know Gabe. He's in the sixth-grade class that's babysitting me the rest of the year."

Vera waves and smiles and says, "Are you the one at her table? The one who doesn't talk?"

I shake my head. "No," I say. "That's Reuben. I talk."

"Oh," Vera says. Then she looks at Rae. "Reuben's the cool one, right?"

Rae nods, and I wrinkle up my forehead and wonder how Reuben could have possibly gotten any cool points.

Then Mr. Jasper says, "OK, we're off," and Rae and

Vera step out of the gazebo. I notice they've changed into hiking boots that tie up over their ankles, and I'm wondering if I'm supposed to have boots. It didn't say that in the registration packet, but maybe that's something outdoorsy Nature Club people just know and I should ask my mom to put that on the list of things I'll need to survive on the trail this summer.

"This is it?" I ask. "This is the whole Nature Club?"

Mr. Jasper nods and gestures toward the remaining daypack on the bench. "You've got a lot to catch up on. We've been practicing orienteering." Then the girls follow him off the gazebo and through the parking lot toward the woods that surround our schoolyard.

I grab the pack and walk fast to keep up. "You've been practicing *what*?" I say.

Rae calls back, "Orienteering. It's like finding your way through the forest."

We stop at the edge of the woods, where Mr. Jasper says, "A new entry point this time, girls." Then he turns toward me. "Today, you'll follow Vera and Rae as they navigate to the checkpoint."

I raise my eyebrows.

"You'll catch on quickly, and they'll give you tips along the way," he says. Then he nods toward my bag. I open it and take out binoculars and a compass, a whistle, and a laminated map with a red-markered dot colored on it. He points to the dot. "That's where you're going."

"Is there a trail?" I ask.

He smiles and shakes his head. "No trails out here."

"Blazes painted on the trees?" I ask.

He shakes his head again. "But you've got Vera and Rae and a compass and a map."

"What's the whistle for?"

He smiles. "In case you get lost."

Then he gives us a wave, says, "Good luck," and walks along the grass near the edge of the woods.

"Where are *you* going?" I call.

He bends over and picks up a stick from the ground, tries it out for size, and starts hiking into the forest. "Exploring," he calls over his shoulder.

Rae holds out her map in one hand. "You keep it with north at the top," she says, and I want to tell her I already know my directions. Never Eat Soggy Waffles. But now she's laying the compass on top of the map, adjusting the face of it, and walking her body slowly in a circle. "This is how you orient your map to the land," she says. "So you know which way you're going."

"Right," I say.

She stops when she's facing the playground, points, and says, "That's north."

Vera flips her map upside down and taps her finger on a line. "This will be our first landmark." Then she's measuring things out with her fingers in little sections across the lines, and she reaches over and turns my map.

"Right," I say again.

Rae wraps the shoelace hanging from the end of the compass around her wrist three times and holds the face of the compass in her palm. "Ready?" she asks.

I wrap my compass like that, too, then nod and follow them into the woods.

I've been going to school in this building since kindergarten, and I've never been in these woods. The woods behind my house and the ones that lead into town have trails where people ride their bikes, walk, and let their dogs run off their leashes. But in here there are no trails, no paths, no way to tell where you're supposed to be going at all. It's just trees and trees and trees, and trees that have fallen over, and trees that are leaning on other trees, and mud and leaves and sticks and roots, and trees. No blazes to let you know you're on the right track, no neighbors running with their dogs to let you know you haven't wandered far from civilization, nothing.

"We want to be going southwest," Vera says.

Rae's checking her compass, then looking down at the map like she knows exactly how it's going to lead us to that red dot.

They take a few steps deeper into the woods and then

stop. They're just standing there, looking one way, then another, through the trees. Then they squat and hold out their arms and close one eye and look down the length of their fingers like they can will a path to appear. No path appears.

"What are you doing?" I ask.

"Watching," Vera says.

"And listening," says Rae.

Watching and *listening* isn't feeling very hiker-explorer-toughening-me-up-to-get-me-ready-for-the-Appalachian-Trail, and I didn't even know mosquitoes came out this early, but I swear there's one buzzing in my ear, and I'm about ready to be done with Nature Club. But I know I can't quit.

"What's at that red dot on the map anyway?" I ask. "Why do we want to go there?"

I'm thinking it better be a pot of gold. Or a mountain of books.

"Not sure until we find it," Vera answers. Then they take off through the trees with their compasses out-stretched, stopping to point their binoculars toward the treetops and whispering names like *field sparrow* and *hermit thrush*. We step on big rocks through a muddy area, and I have to dodge roots and push branches out of my face, and every couple of minutes Vera and Rae

check the map and point and nod and look at their compasses and start off again.

We have to climb over a huge fallen-down tree, and
the way they do it makes it look easy, but when I try, I
can't quite get my leg high enough and kind of have to
hop on my other foot a few times, and then I'm sitting on
the tree like it's a horse and I feel a little stuck, and I'm
pretty sure I pulled a muscle. I shimmy down feetfirst,
and the bark on the tree lifts up my shirt and scrapes
the skin on my back. I hobble over roots that push up
out of the ground, walk too close to a pricker bush and
get burrs stuck all over my shorts, and my left sneaker
sinks down in a soppy mud patch, leaving a deep print
behind. I get the point of the boots now.

We make a few more curves around trees and more
trees, and after what feels like thirty-five miles, they
stop and Vera says, "It should be right here."

Vera looks up and Rae looks down. They start
turning over big rocks and running their hands along
thick tree branches above their heads. Then Rae spots
something beneath an arched root sticking up from the
ground and says, "Found it!"

They rush over and pull out a small tin box, then find
a log for us all to sit on. Rae snaps open the latch, and
inside the tin there are three fun-size packs of M&M'S
and a note.

You found me again
Can't say that I'm shocked
It's a long way that you've come,
A far way that you've walked.

You had a compass,
A map, and good weather,
But most importantly,
You did it together.

You followed your brain,
Your heart, and your feet.
Now please enjoy
This chocolaty treat.
—Tin Bin

"Tin Bin?" I ask.

Vera takes one of the packs of M&M'S out and shakes the container. "We're always looking for Tin Bin," she says. "And he always leaves us something."

Rae hands me a pack of M&M'S and I reach out for it, but really I'm thinking, *We did all that for this? There are like five M&M'S in a fun size.* But when I empty the pack into my mouth and the melty candy shells touch my tongue, it tastes better than M&M'S ever have.

Before I can even swallow the chocolaty clump, Rae

holds out a hand and says, "Wrappers." Vera and I hand over the M&M'S wrappers, and Rae puts them back in Tin Bin. "Leave no trace," she says.

"What's that?" I ask.

"It means, leave the forest the way you found it," she says. "And don't go messing it up with your garbage." She snaps Tin Bin closed and slides it into her daypack.

Then Vera looks down at her map and compass and says, "Better start heading back."

Back? I'm thinking. I hadn't even thought about back. But they stand up from the log and hold their compasses out over their maps again. Then they take a step in the direction we just came from, twigs snapping beneath their boots as they hike off through the trees.

I'm sweating and huffing when we hop across the deep footprint I left in the mud patch, pass the bending-over pricker bush where I got my shorts stuck, and climb over the log where I scraped my back, and I'm trying to think of anything but how much my legs burn from all the stepping, and my brain starts drifting to Reuben and why he's the cool one, and before I know it I huff out, "How do you know Reuben is cool?"

Rae thinks for a second. "He just is. He's chill. Maybe even too chill, because if I were him, no one would be laughing along with that kid Chaz, who thinks he's so funny."

We keep walking, and my face is all sorts of red, and I don't think it's just from the hike.

Right before we reach the end, Vera points beneath some soggy leaves at a candy wrapper crumpled into the mud. Rae pushes back the leaves and grabs the plastic.

I'm thinking that's not even ours, and then I'm thinking that Rae must be some sort of mind reader because she says, "The thing about leave no trace is that it's not just about not messing it up with your own garbage, but also about keeping other people's garbage from messing it up too. If you see it, you're responsible for it."

Then she crumples the wrapper and sticks it in her daypack.

Mr. Jasper meets us at the woods' edge where we started, and he gives us all fist bumps, and Vera hands him Tin Bin. "Great teamwork," he tells us. Then he turns to me. "So, what do you think of Nature Club?"

I'm not really sure what I think of it. I thought it would be different. I thought it would be easier. I thought the M&M'S were amazing. But the words that actually come out of my mouth are, "There were so many trees."

The girls laugh, and so does Mr. Jasper.

"And everything looked the same in there," I continue. "Every direction was just trees and roots and logs and trees and trees."

Mr. Jasper smiles, and we start walking back toward

the gazebo. "That's the whole point of orienteering," he says. "It's about finding yourself. Finding yourself in a place where everything looks familiar and it's hard to tell anything apart."

"Like through a zillion trees," I say.

"Like through a zillion trees," he agrees.

Mr. Jasper tells us to leave all the gear in the day-packs, and I can see Oliver dribbling his basketball hard into the court. He looks over and waves at me, so I hold the binoculars up to my eyes and pretend I'm search-ing the court for him. When I catch him through the lenses, it seems like he's standing one inch in front of me, waving a huge hand right in my face. I can see the individual drops of sweat on his forehead, and his eyes are so big that he almost looks sad.

I pretend I've just seen an Oliver-monster, so I drop the binoculars and jump back and laugh and wave to him. He looks normal from here, not all big-eyed and sad.

He laughs and does this funny little squat and hand gesture from behind. *Did you poop in the woods?* And I have to swallow my giggles as I listen to Mr. Jasper talking about all the stuff he noticed in the woods today. Things like sap, and buds, and a surprise he'll show us next time. Vera and Rae *ooh* and *aah* and start guess-ing, but I don't have any guesses, and club is over, and I'm excited to get to the bookstore, so I zip the map and compass in the pack and leave it on the gazebo bench. By the time I look up again all the Sports Club kids are walking toward the locker room or the parking lot, but I don't see Oliver anymore, and if I wait more than a few minutes for him, my phone will start buzzing and my mom will send out the FBI.

I kick the mud out of my sneakers, fasten my helmet, and hop on my bike. As I ride to the bookstore I see kids walking in groups toward town. Chaz and Orin and Saunders are standing together like a wall at the crosswalk, waiting for the guard to tell them they can go. I stop behind them so I don't have to think of anything to say. They're all laughing, and Chaz says, "But why does he just stand and stare at everyone all recess? It's like he's some secret agent."

That makes Orin laugh so hard he doubles over.

"He's reconnaissance Reuben!" Chaz says. "Recon Reuben!"

"What the heck does that mean?" Saunders asks.

"Recon?" Chaz says; he stops laughing a little. "It's like what the military does when they're trying to get information about their enemy. You know. Like studying or spying."

Saunders and Orin both burst out laughing. "Was that your nerd-word of the day from your mom?" Orin asks.

"Shut up," Chaz says. "It's not even that hard of a word."

But then he pretends to laugh along with them again, and they start talking about how Reuben was probably sent here to study our playground behaviors, and at any second we're going to get ambushed by a group of jungle-gym-hating forces determined to take away our recess.

"He's totally a spy," Chaz says.

A little laugh is growing in my guts thinking about a playground-abolishing militia flying into our schoolyard, and I'm imagining it like a comic in my head, but the laugh turns to gobbledygook because *Recon Reuben* is another name, another story, told behind his back. And because maybe Rae is right; maybe Reuben is the cool one and everyone needs to quit laughing along.

The guard walks out with her stop sign, and everyone starts moving across the street and up the sidewalk. I stand up on my pedals in the bike lane to power by them quickly, but even when I'm long past, I can still hear their laughter. And I kind of wish I were back in the woods.

12.

REUBEN

I KNOW KIDS LIKE Chaz and Orin and Saunders. They're at every school I've been to. Which is a lot.

13.

I'M AT MY LOCKER the next morning when I first hear it. *Recon Reuben creeps around people's houses.*

Jolene is whispering to Corey. "Lenny told me that Gabe and Oliver saw him when they were babysitting some kids. He was just lurking around upstairs."

I close my locker, and Corey says, "There's Gabe. Ask him."

Jolene and Corey rush over, and I can see Lenny and Fiona walking up behind them. "Is it true?"

"H-He wasn't really lurking around," I say. "I'm not even sure it was him—who told you that?"

"Oliver," says Lenny.

"He did? Why would he . . ."

Then Chaz comes over and says, "Gabe and Oliver

are babysitters?" A few kids in the hallway laugh along with him and say things like, "You actually want to wipe noses? And butts?" But then it seems like everyone is just whispering about *Recon Reuben* again, *creeping and spying* and *He better not come in my house!* and *Do you think that's why he moved here? To spy on how other families work, since his left him in an underground prison?* And I'm feeling pretty relieved that they aren't laughing about me being a babysitter anymore, but then that makes me feel even more rotten.

I'm looking for Oliver but he's not by his locker, so I walk down past the office and check in the lunchroom. He's not there, and he's not in the lobby, and there aren't any other places we're allowed to be in the morning before the bell rings. But when I'm passing by the gym back toward my locker again, I hear a ball bouncing, so I try the door and see Oliver dribbling around a fake defender and going up for a shot. He misses and slams the ball hard against the wall. It bounces and rolls to my feet.

"Hi," I say. "I don't think we're supposed to be in here."

"Well, I have to practice."

I pick up the ball, and he puts his hands out to catch my pass, but I just hold it for a second. "Did you tell Lenny that Reuben was in Knox and Kobe's house?"

Oliver squinches up his face and looks at the ceiling like he's trying to remember. "Not really," he says. "I asked him if he knew whether Reuben had brothers. He said how was he supposed to know, and why was I wondering in the first place?" Oliver claps his hands once and puts them out again to receive my pass. "So then I told him you thought you saw him in the window when we were babysitting."

"Oliver!"

"What?"

"Now everyone is saying stuff about him. That he lurks around people's houses and spies on them."

I have so much gobbledygook in my guts I could puke.

And I can tell just by looking at Oliver that he feels bad, too, and I'm expecting him to say he's sorry or he'll fix it or something, but instead he shakes his head and says, "Well, maybe if he doesn't want people talking about him, he should do something about it."

He gestures for the ball again, and I throw it to him. He sinks a shot, then picks up his book bag and walks toward the door. On the way to Ms. Leavitt's room I follow a half step behind Oliver, wondering if he's right, if Reuben should just tell everyone to shut up, and if he is right, why I still feel so rotten.

And I'm wishing I had just asked Reuben myself yesterday. Just been brave enough to walk over to him, ask him if he was Knox and Kobe's brother, let him nod his head or pass me a note or something. Instead, there's another story about Reuben hissing through our halls.

And it's my fault.

Ms. Leavitt meets us at the door and tells us to get ready for *Moment of Meditation*. Saunders comes by our table as I'm taking out my notebook and says, "So is it true you saw Reuben roaming around some kids' house?"

"No," I say.

"Jolene said that Oliver said that you saw him roaming around in a window or something." And before I can even think of what to say, Lenny mutters, "Roaming Reuben." And I know it's going to stick. Rude Reuben. Recon Reuben. Roaming Reuben.

Then Saunders and Orin move on to their table with Chaz, and when I sit down Oliver scooches over and whispers, "I didn't mean to start a rumor."

"I know," I say. But he did. Or did I?

Ms. Leavitt closes the door and says, "Good morning, everyone." She's doing the attendance quietly, her eyes looking up from her clipboard occasionally to check if we're all here. Rae comes in quickly, just in time, and sits next to Reuben.

Then Ms. Leavitt says she's going to start the timer, and we all bend our heads over our desks and begin. Cass is tapping out quiet beats on her table and jotting in her notebook, Jade is drawing a border of doodles with complicated vines and flowers around her paper, and Corey is inking his finger with a black marker, pressing it onto his paper, and making characters out of the prints. Oliver is hiding his phone in his lap again, scrolling, and jotting in his notebook. He doesn't look up when Ms. Leavitt whispers, "This is halftime." We're supposed to be switching notebooks, but he tells me his TV is still broken and he wants to catch up on the NBA scores.

I'm looking at Reuben, and feeling gobbledygook, and thinking about how quickly a story can fly around a room, and how I wish I could go back and change my part. But I wasn't brave enough to just ask Reuben myself, to talk to him in front of my whole class, and I don't even know why. Except that no one talks to him. We just talk about him.

I feel my shoulders sink, and Ms. Leavitt tells us to wrap up our last thoughts, so I tap my pen on my paper and write.

Redo
Undo
My
One
Reaction

Rae is sitting with the two blank papers in front of her. "I'm still not apologizing," she says as Ms. Leavitt walks by her table.

"I'm sure you'll find the right words," Ms. Leavitt says, and gives her a little smile and nod. That makes Rae smile, too, and then she scoots her chair closer to the table and taps the eraser of her pencil a few times on the first blank page.

Then I hear Chaz whisper to Saunders, "I bet Roaming Reuben's been in her house too." And a few kids try to hide their laughs in their elbows.

"What's that supposed to mean?" Rae asks. But she doesn't ask Chaz; she asks Reuben, who shrugs and takes a minute to write something to her in his notebook. She reads it and rolls her eyes. "Name-calling and rumor starting," she mutters. "Real cool."

Chaz smacks his teeth and mumbles, "Whatever," and I look away fast because I'm thinking about leaving no trace and wondering if I've tossed garbage in Reuben's path and now I don't know how to clean it up.

Rae taps each blank piece of paper once with her eraser. "Which one should I start with?" she asks. "English teacher for the bad word, or Principal Tacker for not giving her my cell phone?"

Reuben raises his eyebrows.

"Don't worry," she says. "They're not going to be apology letters, exactly." Reuben points to the first page.

"English teacher," she says. "Good choice."

Ms. Leavitt is calling for our attention and telling us that time is up for our *Moment of Meditation* and to switch gears to working on our projects. The NBA games must be really important and interesting because I have to nudge Oliver.

He zips his phone in his book bag and says, "All right. *Gabiver* time."

The first frame of our comic is almost done. Oliver drew the whole playground with the swings and slides, and the teeter-totter is right in the middle next to the sandbox. "I just need to add us now," he says. Then he starts sketching the pre-K version of himself, with his sisters' hand-me-down pink fleece jacket and light-up sparkle sneakers, sitting on the down side of the teeter-totter.

I'm drafting the thought and speech balloons and remembering how Oliver said, "Climb on. We can do it together."

And how I was thinking *No way*, but instead I said, "Yeah, OK."

And how when I fell off, I was thinking, *That's it. I'm done,* but then he said, "Get back on. Try again." So I did. Sometimes you need a friend like Oliver.

Even though I'm writing I'm also kind of eavesdropping on Ms. Leavitt, who's kneeling next to Reuben. My first thought is that I hope he isn't telling her that I'm the one responsible for starting the newest rumor, because I don't want her getting up from his table, coming to ours, and giving me her look.

But what she's actually saying is, "Remember what I told you about this project, Reuben." And she goes on about how she knows it's hard to adjust to a new school, especially toward the end of the year, and that she doesn't expect him to hand in a polished project. All that makes me feel even more rotten for hoping I wasn't about to get in trouble, because I never even really thought about how it must be hard moving schools. I've never had to do that. And I wonder if Reuben has an Oliver back wherever he came from.

Ms. Leavitt stands up and says to Reuben, "You can use this time observing any of your classmates if that's helpful. I'm sure they'd be happy to talk you through what they're working on, and maybe it'll give you some ideas."

Chaz whispers that Reuben gets away with everything, he doesn't have to talk, and now he doesn't have to do the project. Someone else whispers, "Recon Reuben would love to observe," and there are a few giggles.

I don't think Ms. Leavitt hears the comments or the

giggles, because she doesn't say anything, and when Reuben points to the roll of bulletin paper in the back of the room, she says, "Sure," and helps him rip off a piece. It doesn't rip cleanly and leaves a long, jagged edge on one side, but when Ms. Leavitt goes to get scissors to help him even it out, Reuben holds the paper up in both hands, looks at it for what seems like a whole minute, and then shakes his head at the scissors. And I'm wondering why you would want to do a project on a piece of paper that looks like that, square and even on one side and the other stretching out all ragged like long zags of lightning.

Andre is tapping beats on his desk with his fingers as he writes his poems in his notebook, and Ms. Leavitt lets Cass bring her guitar to class and sit in the walk-in supply closet in the back of the room.

Chaz is opening and closing a big cardboard box that's on his desk. It has a picture of winter boots on the outside and a bunch of loose paper on the inside, but so far it doesn't look like he's doing anything with it. And I'm wondering if maybe this time he's not going to write some thousand-page essay that Principal Tacker will want him to read over the loudspeaker.

Oliver nudges my elbow and slides the first frame of our comic toward me. It's perfect. In the picture he's sitting on the bottom of the teeter-totter, his knees bent up to his ears. I'm standing next to the swings with a sand-box truck in my hand, looking at him. And I don't even know why, but my eyes start to burn and my throat feels tight like I could cry at any second because I'm so glad I got on that teeter-totter, and so glad his mom was late to pick him up so we could find a rhythm, and so glad we have a teacher cool enough to let us make a comic for our project. I blink hard and tell him it's great, and he slides a case of colored pencils toward me.

We compare a couple of shades of blue and decide on bright, sky blue for the teeter-totter. And I find a perfect pink for Oliver's fleece jacket and silver for his light-up sneakers.

Then I pull out the black pencil and start writing the thought and speech bubbles in the neatest handwriting I can.

By the end of the period we have a complete, colored first frame and we're talking about the next one, a close-up of us both on the teeter-totter laughing.

The bell rings, and I slide our papers into the folder to keep them flat. Chaz asks Ms. Leavitt if he can store his box in the classroom. She says, "Sure."

And I'm thinking this is maybe the first time Chaz isn't bringing a project home to work extra on it, because when Cass comes out of the supply closet with her guitar he goes in and tucks the box on a high shelf and pushes it all the way to the back.

Reuben folds his bulletin board paper right down the middle and slides it into his book bag, and I'm wondering what he's working on, and I'm thinking that maybe tomorrow I'll tell him that he can observe us working on our *Gabiver* project if he wants.

When we get to math, there's another woman standing with Ms. Myers at the front of the room, and Oliver and I are still talking one hundred miles per hour about the next frame for our comic. But when we sit down, Oliver stuffs his book bag beneath the desk and starts digging through it like he's lost something.

"You OK?" I ask.

"Fine," he says, and sticks even more of his body down beneath his desk to rummage through his stuff.

"I'd like to crawl through a book bag portal away from math too," I say, but it doesn't make him laugh, and Ms. Myers is clapping for our attention.

She introduces us to her friend, who is a real estate agent, and says, "She uses the math we've been studying this year every day in her job to help people buy and sell their houses."

Then she passes out a worksheet with *Buying a House* printed on top. When she gets to our table, Ms.

Myers puts her hand on Oliver's shoulder. "Head up, please," she whispers.

Oliver lifts his head, but then he looks down and puts his hand over his face like he's trying to block his eyes from the sun.

"Are you sure you're OK?" I ask.

He nods, and then the real estate agent kind of looks at him funny and says, "You're . . . Oliver?"

Everyone looks at Oliver, and his eyes get big, and I can see the little muscles bulging from tightening his jaw so hard.

"Oh," Ms. Myers says. "I didn't know you two . . ."

"She knows my mom from the restaurant," Oliver says. "She's a regular on my mom's shifts." Then he asks if he can go to the bathroom, and Ms. Myers says sure and to be quick, which makes everyone laugh because that's his name. Oliver Quick.

The real estate agent uses the whiteboard to explain how a down payment works, and Ms. Myers says, "Remember how we've been working on percent?" Then we try a few problems from the worksheet on our own, and I'm wondering if these numbers are true. If houses actually cost $200,000 or $350,000, because I don't know what I was expecting, but these numbers seem really, really big.

The real estate agent says most people don't have that much money, which is why there's this thing called a down payment and a loan for the rest. I'm moving the decimal to find ten percent and multiplying by two so I can find the down payment, like Ms. Myers taught us, and even those numbers seem big, but really I'm wondering what's taking Oliver so long.

And a few minutes later Ms. Myers is wondering, too, because she asks me if I'll go check on him.

Both bathrooms in the middle school wing are empty, and there's no one at the water fountain. He's not at his locker, and I even check back in Ms. Leavitt's room, but the door's locked and the lights are off. I stop in the elementary wing's bathroom, too, but there's only one person in there, and when I bend down to see beneath the stalls I see purple high-top sneakers, which isn't what Oliver wears.

Ms. Myers gets a worried look on her face when I tell her I didn't find him and picks up her classroom phone, which I'm pretty sure can only call one place, Principal Tacker's office.

A bunch of whispers sneak around the room, and Chaz says something about how Oliver's probably making a break for it. Orin laughs, and Ms. Myers is watching the door, and I accidentally catch Reuben's eyes, and he doesn't need a speech balloon stretching over his head to say he's sad.

It feels like forever, but it's only five minutes later that Principal Tacker opens the door and Oliver walks in behind her. "Seems Mr. Quick got lost," she says. Chaz laughs, and Reuben takes a deep breath and lets it go.

I have a thousand questions like, *Are you OK? Where were you? Are you in trouble with Principal Tacker?* but the bell rings and Ms. Myers asks us to finish the rest of the worksheet at home, and Oliver packs up fast, and we walk out of the room with our shoulders pressed together.

14.

REUBEN

I USED TO HIDE in bathroom stalls. I'd stand on the toilet seat so no one could see my sneakers.

Until recess was over.

My principal found me there one afternoon and told my mom maybe I'd do better with a new school. A fresh start.

This is my third new school.

My third fresh start.

15.

MY MOM ALWAYS REMINDS me that we have to ride single file on our bikes, even if there aren't any cars on the street, but I want to zoom up next to Oliver and ask him about where he went for such a long time during math class. So I look quickly behind me to check for cars and pedal up next to him.

"Hey," I say. "Where'd you go during math?"

He stands up on his pedals and gets his wheel out a little ahead of mine. "The gym was unlocked, so I was practicing my free throws," he says. "Until Principal Tacker showed up and asked me what I thought I was doing there and took the ball."

"Taker," I say.

He laughs and says, "Exactly."

He keeps pedaling hard and inching ahead. We're on our way to Knox and Kobe's, and I don't want to be late, because I'm trying to be responsible, but I also don't want to be early, because I know I can't do one minute more than two hours with those two.

Oliver and I took our time after school, packing up slowly at our lockers and sharing the crackers and string cheese my mom packed for snack. Then after all the buses left we walked slowly to our bikes. But if he's going to be standing up on his pedals and cruising like this, I think we'll still be early.

I pull up next to him again. "That was really your mom's friend?" I ask.

"Who?"

"The real estate lady, from math. The one who knew you." I stand up on my pedals and am huffing to stay with him.

"Oh, not really," he says. He's pedaling and pedaling, and my legs are burning to keep up. "She just comes in on my mom's shift sometimes and has seen me there, too, so she thinks we're best friends now."

I laugh and say, "Well, that position is unfortunately already taken."

"Exactly," Oliver says, and I sink back behind him to turn on to Knox and Kobe's street. And as we coast to their house I'm thinking that it has never once occurred to me to just not go to class and do whatever I felt like instead, which would be read about Dog Man in the back window seat of the library all day. But I also didn't think just not going to class would ever cross Oliver's mind either. And I know he's serious about basketball, but it's like someone just told him he could try out for the NBA or something and now he has to practice all the time.

Knox and Kobe are out in their driveway riding matching tricycles. One of them has a wheel stuck in the mud and can't get it to roll. He's starting to whine and slams his fists against the handlebars, but then he sees us coming and points.

Both kids hop off the trikes and run toward the street. Paula catches them by the hoods of their sweatshirts before they reach the curb.

"Gabe! Oyiver!" they shout.

Paula puts in her earbuds and waves. "See you at five thirty," she says, and jogs back toward the house. I check the upstairs window, but Reuben isn't there, and I'm thinking it was probably my imagination, and now there's a *Roaming Reuben* rumor creeping through our school for no reason.

My watch says it's three twenty-six, and I can't believe we have four extra minutes to fill. The boys run up and hug us around the knees while we drop our bikes in the yard. I check the left pointer finger of one. "Kobe," I say. He's wearing green today, and Knox is wearing purple, so I try to remember *Kobe-green-Kobe-green-Kobe-green.*

Oliver unclips his helmet and says, "What do you want to do today?"

"Eat yoyipop!" Kobe squeals.

"Yoyipop!" Knox echoes.

"No lollipops," I tell them. "Not today."

Their lips start to quiver. "But we yike yoyipops," Knox whines.

"Paint?" says Kobe.

I'm thinking that sounds like a terrible idea, but Oliver says, "OK," before I can say *No way.* And Knox and Kobe take us by the hands and lead us into the house.

We help them out of their shoes, and Kobe unzips his green sweatshirt and flings it through the mudroom and across the kitchen. Now I have to change my mantra. *Kobe-dragon-T-shirt-Kobe-dragon-T-shirt.*

There are big squeezy bottles of finger paints on a shelf in the playroom, and Kobe opens the toy chest and takes out a plastic bin with folded, paint-spattered smocks and brushes. We Velcro the smocks behind their necks and tear thick pieces of art paper from their pad. I don't know where to squeeze the paint, and I don't want

136

to use one of the nice dishes from the kitchen, so we decide to put a little squirt on the actual paper.

"Red!" Knox says.

I shake the red bottle and squeeze a little out, but it makes a big *phlpppp* sound.

Both boys look at me, then look at each other and start giggling. "Farted!" Knox says. And they start making spitty fart sounds with their mouths.

"It was the bottle," I tell them. "When air comes out of it . . ."

Oliver's laughing, too, now. "It did sound a little like guano," he says. And now I can't stop laughing either.

We squeeze-fart some more colors onto their papers and let them paint with their fingers. It's not even painting. It's smooshing. They rub the colors around in the same spot in the middle until everything turns brown and the paper starts to get mushy and tear.

Oliver shows them how to make baby footprints, plopping the outside of his fist in purple paint and pressing it on the clean corner of Knox's paper. Then he dots five purple toes with his pointer finger. "See?" he says. "A baby footprint."

"On mine!" Kobe says, and Oliver makes one on his paper too.

Then they both start trying to make their own prints

137

while Oliver goes to wash the paint off his hands in the bathroom.

I'm looking around the room for any evidence that Reuben lives here, but there aren't any family pictures or albums that I can see. Just bookshelves, and toy baskets, and a big framed painting of Vermont's green mountains.

The boys are happy pressing their fingers down, making three- and eight-toed baby footprints. "I'll be right back," I tell them, and walk around the circle into the living room. More bookshelves, more landscape art, but no photos. In the kitchen I see a scribble drawing on the refrigerator with *Knox and Kobe* and a date penciled in the corner. I can tell there's another drawing beneath it, held by the same magnet, so I lift the scribble and see a drawing of a girl.

It looks professional. Wispy pencil sketch lines make the shape of the girl's eyes and her not-smiling, but not-not-smiling mouth. Written on the bottom is *The Listener*, and right as it hits me that I know who she is, I hear Oliver come out of the bathroom and say, "What the . . . ?" but he stops before he says the starts-with-*h* bad word.

I drop the scribble back down over the portrait and rush around the corner to see the boys standing on their chairs and pressing baby footprints up the wall.

"Oh no," I say.

"Yook!" one of them says, and points proudly to their paintings. "Yook we did!"

Oliver rushes past me into the kitchen to rip off a paper towel and run it under the faucet. I help Knox and Kobe down from their chairs and pull them away from the wall as Oliver tries scrubbing, but it's not working. It's smearing. Not disappearing.

"You guys can't paint on the walls!" I say. "Look what you did."

They look up at me, and I watch their eyes fill with tears. "You don't have to cry, though," I say. "It's OK."

"You said we baaaaaad!" one of them says. I can't remember now which was dragon T-shirt. But now they're both crying and wrapping themselves around me.

"I didn't say that," I say. "Please just stop crying. It's OK. We'll clean it."

They squeeze their crinkly smocks into me and hold on tight to my shirt. "Sowwy," one says. The other sniffles.

Oliver wets the paper towels again. Most of it is coming off, but you can still see red and purple smudges like little bruises stretching up the wall, and the kids start up their crying again.

"You were supposed to be watching them," Oliver says. "What were you doing?"

"I-I was looking for . . ."

But before I can finish I hear footsteps coming down the stairs, the sound of the baby gate squeaking open at the bottom, and then he's standing right there in the playroom.

"Weuben!" Knox and Kobe yell.

He's holding a damp sponge and a bottle of something called Soft Scrub that he sprays on the smudges. Then he wipes slow circles on the wall until the stains are gone, and looks right at us and shakes his head because we can't even be trusted with three squeezy-farty bottles of kids' paint.

I feel awkward. It's the same feeling I had when I was at the grocery store with Mom after school one day and we saw Ms. Leavitt. Like we shouldn't be seeing her there, because she belonged at school, and I couldn't imagine her cooking dinner and eating food, and I didn't have any idea what to say.

I don't know what to say now either. Because Reuben belongs sitting silently at the table near the classroom library or pressed against the bricks in the shadow of the building during recess, and it feels strange to imagine him living in a house and cleaning a stain and drawing a picture that someone hangs on the refrigerator.

Knox and Kobe stop crying when they see the clean wall, and they leave me to wrap themselves around him. Reuben pats their heads with his free hand, and when the twins finally pull away from him, I see their handprints and smock smudges all over Reuben's white T-shirt. He looks down at his paint-smeared shirt, and then at us, and rolls his eyes and shrugs. Then he points to my shirt, which is also swiped with purple and red, and huffs a little laugh. I roll my eyes and shrug too.

"He's bruvver," one of them says.

"We know Reuben," I tell them. "He's in our class at school."

"He is?"

"Yup," I say. Then I kind of smile and nod at Reuben, hoping he knows that I'm trying to tell him *Thanks, for the wall.*

He nods back and waves bye and heads back upstairs.

"That was weird," Oliver mutters to me when he's gone.

And before I can say *yeah*, one of the twins says, "Not weird."

And the other says, "Weuben."

Oliver laughs a little and goes to throw away his wad of paper towels.

I check behind the kid's left pointer fingers and say, "Kobe." He nods. I study his face for a minute, and then I look to Knox. "Maybe you two are right," I whisper. "Maybe it's not so weird."

* * *

We sit on the playroom couch and read three books about the same construction site over and over one thousand times, and we get through the rest of the two hours without any more messes, poopy diapers, or lollipop meltdowns.

When it's five thirty, Paula comes up from the basement, takes out her earbuds, and searches through her wallet while Knox and Kobe wrap themselves around each of her ankles. She doesn't have the right change again, and I tell her it's OK, she overpaid us last time, so she can pay us less today. But Oliver shoots me a look, and she waves us off and gives us each twenty dollars again.

We thank her, and she says she'll see us next time, and I'm hoping she doesn't notice any weird smudges on the playroom wall, and when we hop on our bikes to head home, I want to tell Oliver about the sketch I saw on their refrigerator. How it looked professional, how it could be in a museum, and it even had a title, and how he got Rae's sticky-uppy hair and bandanna exactly right.

I'm supposed to tell Oliver everything. We're Gabiver. I'm supposed to have a joke about how maybe Reuben *is* K-I-S-S-I-N-G Rae, and we're supposed to come up with a reason for why Reuben can't watch his own brothers.

But this time, it feels like I should just be quiet.

I wave bye to Oliver and tell him I'll see him tomorrow, and I start pedaling home. My heart is beating, and fast, and I'm wondering if Reuben *talks* to Rae. Why else would he call her *the listener*?

16.

REUBEN

I WILL NEVER BE a babysitter.

Not even for Knox and Kobe.

Not a chance.

If I've learned anything, it's that I need to stay out of the way, and keep my mouth shut, so no one gets hurt.

Or worse.

17.

THERE'S A NOTE ON the kitchen counter the next morning in Dad's loopy handwriting.

> *Gabe,*
> *Sorry I'll miss breakfast.*
> *Got called in for Rosalie. This might be it.*
> *I know she's your favorite. That makes sense.*
> *You're a lot alike. She's the real deal, Gabe.*
> *And you're both funny as hell.*
> *See ya tomorrow for Corn Pops.*
> *—Dad*

My eyes are a little watery because even though I never met Rosalie she really was my favorite. And from the way Dad describes it, I'm not the only one who felt that way. She was kind and open to everyone, she was funny, and even though her liver was sick, Dad said there wasn't one thing wrong with that heart of hers. I guess that's what being the real deal is.

Mom comes in and puts her arm around my shoulders. "He shouldn't have said *h-e-l-l*," she says.

"He didn't," I say. "He wrote it."

Mom laughs.

"See? He's right," I say. "I *am* funny as . . ."

Mom squeezes my shoulder hard like *Don't you dare*, but she's still kind of laughing. It makes me think of Rae and how she said *h* to her English teacher, but I bet if I explained why, Mom would agree it was an appropriate word for the occasion, just like Rae said.

"I know it's kind of weird," I say. "But I wish I could say something to Rosalie."

"You can," Mom says. "Just say it. Point yourself in the direction of the hospital, here, like this." She rotates my shoulders to the backyard. "And then, say it."

She goes to put some bread in the toaster, leaving me facing out the glass-paned back door.

"It's not like she'll be able to hear me," I say.

Mom pulls the lever down for the toaster until it clicks and says, "Well, there's more than one way to listen."

* * *

I'm trying not to feel awkward when I see Reuben in Ms. Leavitt's class, but it's not working. I can't stop thinking about how we were in his house yesterday, and I can't help wondering what they had for dinner, and if they watched TV later, or if he helps tuck his brothers in at night.

I'm trying not to look at him, but it's hard to tell your brain to not do something because then that's the only thing you can think about doing. So I sneak a quick peek during *Moment of Meditation*. He's bent over his desk, drawing on that jagged piece of bulletin board paper. I can see his hands making quick pencil lines. He's drawing another person, but I can't see who it is, and it makes me think of *The Listener* beneath Knox and Kobe's scribble on their refrigerator, and then I feel awkward all over again that I know what Reuben's refrigerator looks like.

Next to him, Rae is working on her letter, and it's long. She reaches the bottom of the page and turns it over to keep going, and I can tell from the little in-between smile on her face that she likes what she's writing. I wish she had a thought bubble above her head so I could know what she's thinking.

Oliver is sneaking his phone in his lap again, and I'm drawing a stick figure comic of myself standing and facing out the glass door to my backyard. I draw a thought bubble up from my head and write, *Rosalie, I'll be the real deal too*, because even though I didn't say anything out loud when I turned in the direction of the hospital this morning, Mom says there's more than one way to listen, and maybe Rosalie can feel my message somehow.

Ms. Leavitt lets us know that it's time to work on our projects and reminds us that they're due in a week.

We take out our folder, and I start touching up the colors on one frame of our *Gabiver* comic, while Oliver is sketching out the next scene. We have a good system, working like this, and it's a good thing that I'm a righty and Oliver's a lefty, because we can sit shoulder to shoulder over the same comic and still have elbow room.

I'm making my Crocs bright green like they were in pre-K, and I'm coloring my hair a shade lighter than Oliver's. My smile is wide in this picture, which makes my dimples more obvious. I look like I'm really free, flying up and up with Oliver there, keeping me balanced.

I dot dark brown freckles on Oliver's face and realize that in the drawing he's not smiling, and his eyes are looking off toward the parking lot.

I check my notebook for what we decided on the speech balloons. I'm supposed to be saying, *Wheee!* and he's supposed to be saying, *That's it! You've got it now!*

But his face in the drawing isn't saying that.

"You kind of look sad in this one," I say.

Oliver just shrugs and says, "I'll check it out after." He's working on the next frame, where this time he's up in the air on the teeter-totter and I'm down.

Principal Tacker's voice crackles through the loud-speaker, calling Rae to her office. Rae rolls her eyes, packs her book bag, and heads toward the door, mumbling, "This better be about me going back to seventh grade."

We continue working, and then halfway through class, Ms. Leavitt calls for our attention and says she wants us to partner with another person or group for a peer conference. A peer conference is when you team up and share your work. There's a whole chart on the wall about peer conferences and how to be a good sharer, a good listener, and the kinds of questions you can ask to help your peers with their projects.

Chaz turns to Orin, and Cass takes her guitar to Missy and Tonya's table. Oliver looks back at Saunders, but he's already sliding his chair to Jolene's table, and Andre and Corey are sitting together on the rug near the library.

Reuben's just sitting there, watching the door, and I am, too, hoping that Rae will barge in any second and be his partner.

Ms. Leavitt is beginning her countdown, and when she gets to zero, we'll have to start our peer conferences.

"Five," she says.

I know if Reuben gets up to search for a partner someone might call him Recon Reuben or Rude Reuben, and I'm surprised that Ms. Leavitt can't see that, because she's looking back and gesturing for him to go ahead and try to find a group to sit in on.

"Four, three . . . ," she says.

Reuben rolls his eyes and keeps drawing, and Ms. Leavitt makes her way to his table. Maybe she'll kneel down next to him and say it's OK, that he doesn't have to join a conference, but then Chaz will say something about him getting out of it.

"Two . . ."

Then I do a little cough to get Reuben's attention and wave him over.

"What are you doing?" Oliver whispers.

"I don't know," I say.

Reuben sighs and folds his paper and walks with it to our table. I point to the extra chair across from us.

"You can peer conference here," I say. "We're making a comic."

I think I catch him smile a little, and he sits down.

Oliver goes back to sketching, and I point to my

notebook page and tell Reuben how I'm working on the speech balloons for this first scene.

"This is a true story," I tell him. "About how Oliver and I met and became friends."

He looks at the scene and sees the playground, then pushes his chair back an inch like he's on the real playground and wishes he could press into the bricks.

"This is our pre-K teacher, Ms. Carrie," I say, pointing to the comic. "And this is my mom." Then I draw Ms. Carrie a speech balloon and write, *Feel free to take Gabe. I can wait with Oliver for his mom.*

Then I draw my mom's speech balloon and write, *It's OK. What's a teeter without a totter?*

Reuben smiles at that line, and I say, "My mom really said that. She's cool sometimes."

He laughs and makes that sign for *Me too*, moving his hand between us with his thumb and pinky out. We're supposed to use that in class when we agree with someone. I laugh a little because I know his mom and she does seem pretty cool.

And when we're smiling like this, I finally get the guts to ask, "What are you doing for your project?" and I point to the folded bulletin board paper.

He raises his eyebrows and leans over his paper like he's not ready to share anything about it. Then Ms.

Leavitt comes by and puts her hands on the backs of our chairs and says, "Good to see you all working together. If you'd like to move your seat here, Reuben, I'm sure that would be fine with Gabe and Oliver."

When she leaves, Reuben jots a note on the corner of his notebook, rips it off, and slides it over to me: *She thinks if I sit with people, I'll make friends. . . . It doesn't work.*

Then I look at Oliver and shrug, and I write: *It might.*

Reuben shakes his head, and he still doesn't unfold his drawing to share. I put the note in my book bag.

So we just continue on our project, and Reuben watches as Oliver rotates the comic frame and begins drawing the fence around the playground. I start sketching a stick figures draft in my notebook of the next scene. It's the one where we're going to get thrown from the teeter-totter, and when we collide in midair the school nurse will rush out to save us the only way she can: stitch us together into *Gabiver*!

Reuben pushes his chair back even farther. Then he nods and goes back to his table, and I'm not sure why, because I thought he liked our comic, and I even kind of liked talking to him about it. But he opens his own drawing and gets back to work.

Rae comes back in and announces that Principal

Tacker is now going to be checking the progress of her letters, and Ms. Leavitt puts her hand on Rae's shoulder and says, "Think of it as a not-so-peer conference." That makes everyone laugh.

On the way to math, Chaz catches us in the hall and says, "Ms. Leavitt must have heard you guys are babysitters. How much is she paying you to watch Reuben in class?" He smacks Oliver and me across the backs like we're in on some big joke, and at first I kind of laugh along. But the cool points turn to gobbledygook in my guts, and I'm trying to say *No, that's not what it's like.* But then Chaz continues, "Or is he joining your group or something?" Chaz's laughs are loud, and now Jolene and Jade are giggling about us being babysitters, and before I know it, Oliver's responding instead.

"He's not in our group now," he says. "That would be kind of weird." Then he tightens the straps of his book bag before entering Ms. Myers's room.

And I'm remembering what one of the twins said, and so before we go in, I say it to Oliver. "Not weird," I say. "Reuben."

Oliver looks at me and says, "I just meant that it would be weird for him to work on our friendship project. It's about you and me."

And I guess that sort of makes sense, and it feels

good that Oliver just wants me as his best friend, but I still feel gobbledygooky. So I try to figure out which direction the hospital's in, so I know which way to point my shoulders to tell Rosalie that being the real deal is hard, but I don't know which way it is, and I don't have a compass.

18.

REUBEN

THEY THINK I CAN'T hear them making fun.

Or laughing along.

19.

AT THE END OF the day I ask Oliver if he wants to work on *Gabiver* after our clubs. "I could show you the sketch I have for the big collision scene, and we could try to figure out what crime he's going to solve."

Oliver grabs his Sports Club bag out of his locker. "I wish," he says. "But I have to help my mom with something." He slings his bag over his shoulder and closes his locker. "Text me if you get a good idea, though." He wiggles his cell phone in front of his chest.

"Take that, *Taker*!" I say a little too loudly. Principal Tacker is just down the hall, and she clears her throat. Oliver drops his phone down his shirt and crosses his arms over his belly to stop it from falling out of the bottom.

"Mr. Mackey," she says, and everyone in the hall turns and stares. "Don't think I can't hear you." Then she continues on down the hall.

"That was a close one," Oliver says, sliding his phone out from the bottom of his shirt.

I let out a big breath and say, "Yeah."

But really I'm wondering if Principal Tacker has been hearing us call her Taker all year. I thought we'd been keeping it behind her back and beneath our breath, but I guess whispers are never quiet enough, and even when you think people aren't listening, they are.

Mr. Jasper is in the gazebo when I get there, and the daypacks are lined up on the bench. His own pack is already on his back, and there's a big Y-shaped stick tied to the outside of it. It's the wrong shape for a walking stick, and too short, and I'm thinking maybe he's just the kind of nature guy that has to carry a stick with him wherever he goes. Either that or it fell from a tree and got stuck on the bungee straps of his pack and he's just so woodsy that he hasn't even noticed.

Ms. Neely is setting up cones on the soccer field, and the Sports Club kids are circled around and warming up with jumping jacks. The elementary after-school clubs are gathering near the playground, and Vera and Rae are making their way across the field from the school.

As they get closer, I hear Rae say, "You've got to be

kidding me. Really, tell me you're kidding."

My eyes must be asking a question because Rae answers, "Vera just told me that our English teacher boxed up all the graphic novels for the rest of the year to . . ." Rae makes quotes in the air with her fingers. "Encourage more reading across other genres."

"What?" I say. "Graphic novel isn't even a genre. It's a format. And who takes books away to encourage more reading?"

"Exactly," Vera and Rae say at the same time.

Vera shakes her head and says, "And I had just finished *Real Friends*, and now I can't get the next two in the series."

"This deserves more bad words," Rae says.

Mr. Jasper is checking to make sure everything is in the daypacks. Then he looks up. "OK," he says. "Are you all ready to search for something even better than Tin Bin?"

"What's better than Tin Bin?" Vera says, and they both unzip a pack and take out the map.

"I don't know," Rae says. "But we're going to find it right there." She taps her finger on the red dot on the map. "It better be our box of graphic novels."

That makes us laugh, and Mr. Jasper hands me the last daypack. "Ready to make a path?"

I nod and open the pack and remember what Vera

and Rae taught me about laying my compass flat and turning my body to orient the map to the land. "It's this way," I say, and point to the woods behind the basketball court.

Vera gives me a high five, and we all walk around the court, watching the needles on our compasses waver.

Before we duck into the woods I look over toward Sports Club and see Oliver doing some squat-jump exercises, and on his next jump up he shouts, "Don't get lost, Gabe!"

I wave my compass at him and smile back. "Don't pull a muscle!"

Mr. Jasper comes into the woods with us today, but we lead. Rae first, with her compass in one hand and map in the other. Then Vera. Then me. I hold my compass and map just like they do and squint through the branches and then back down at the map, trying to figure out where we are and where we're going.

Rae squats by a huge boulder and looks out through the trees. Then points to the lines on her map. "See here? The land rises." I saw the lines on the maps last time, but I didn't realize what they meant.

I follow her finger over the lines on the map, and then I kneel down beside her and look out to see a little hill sloping in front of us.

"I see it!" I say.

Vera holds out the compass and says, "We want to be going northwest right over the top of that."

Then she says, "Why don't you lead for a little bit, Gabe? We'll follow you."

"That's OK," I say. "I still don't know what all the lines—"

Rae puts her hand on my shoulder. "Just give it a try. We'll be here to guide you back if you go astray."

I look at Mr. Jasper and he nods. I still don't have hiking boots, but I wore taller socks today, so I pull them up to my calves, and then I take a few steps past Rae and Vera and the huge boulder and look out into the woods. I check the needle on my compass and try to keep it on northwest as I walk toward the hill. Sticks snap beneath my sneakers, and my shirt catches on a branch sticking out from a tree. I unhook it and try to remember what Mr. Jasper said on Monday about finding yourself in a place where everything looks familiar and it's hard to tell anything apart. He's right. Every direction I turn looks the same. Tall trees.

But I fix my eyes on the ground and just keep on going.

After a minute Vera says, "Gabe."

I look back.

"Check your compass."

The needle has moved. Now it's hovering over west.

"Weird," I say. "It felt like I was going straight."

Rae nods. "It's easy to get pulled off course," she says. "It just takes one tiny step, then another. You don't even realize you're doing it."

I hold out my compass and turn my body until the needle slides back to northwest. Then Mr. Jasper taps me under the chin. "Keep that head up," he says. "And look three steps out in front of you. That's how you plan your path."

He points to the ground three steps in front of me, slightly up the hill. "You have to know where you're going to plant your foot before you get there."

I see dirt and leaves and a thick root pushing up out of the ground. I decide I'll step on the flat ground right before that root. Then on the flat ground right after.

"And when things go wrong?" Mr. Jasper asks, quizzing the girls.

"Stop and accept the fact that you don't know where you are," Rae says.

"And backtrack to the last place you were sure about," Vera adds.

I look back down the hill to the boulder where I took the lead. "There," I say.

"You're lucky your anchor point is still in sight. Now correct your path and look ahead," Mr. Jasper says. He points northwest into the trees, and I keep my eyes up the hill as I hike, planning my trail three steps ahead until we reach what feels like the top of the hill and I stop.

"We're right here," Rae says, and points to a line on my map. "Top of the hill."

Then she runs her finger northwest across the lines and numbers on my map and toward the red dot. "Down we go."

She takes the lead this time, and Mr. Jasper reminds me not to just follow her footsteps. "Keep looking ahead," he says. "And checking your map and compass."

After a couple of minutes we get to the bottom of the hill, and we all check our compasses and hold them over the maps. "We need to walk more north now," Vera says, and takes the lead. "We should be close."

After a minute she stops.

"Are we there?" I ask.

"I don't know," she says. "But it smells different right here."

Mr. Jasper smiles.

"And it sounds different too," Rae adds. "Not so dry and crunchy."

"Good observations," Mr. Jasper says.

Now I'm back to thinking that Nature Club is some kind of dandelion-puff club because they're taking deep breaths and not moving a muscle.

"Check this out," Mr. Jasper says. He squats down and runs his finger through the mud like it's chocolate frosting, holding it up for us to see.

"Mud," Vera says.

Duh, I'm thinking.

"And animal tracks." He points his muddy finger to prints on the ground. "And scat."

"What's scat?" I ask.

"Animal poop," Rae says, and it immediately sends giggles up from my belly because I'm thinking about Oliver and dirty diapers and guano.

Then before I know it, Mr. Jasper pulls the Y-shaped stick from his pack and grips each of the sides in an underhanded fist with the bottom of the Y slightly tipped and pointing out like an airplane taking off.

"What are you doing?" Vera asks.

"I've seen this on TV!" Rae says.

Mr. Jasper starts walking, quietly, back and forth across the dirt and mud. He ducks beneath branches full of green leaves and along low-lying shrubs. He holds the Y steady out over the land the whole time, and then he takes another step, and the stick, still tight between his fists, points down to a spot on the ground like it's found an answer.

"Here," he says.

Then he kneels down and begins digging a wide

circle, clearing away leaves and rocks. He digs and digs a little bowl into the earth, and right before my eyes, water starts bubbling out of the ground like someone buried a fountain in there and it's filling up the bowl.

"A spring!" Vera says.

"This is awesome!" says Rae.

"Wait," I say. "Did that stick just find water?"

Mr. Jasper laughs. "Hotly debated," he says. "Some say water dowsing is luck and baloney. But some say there's a little bit of energy in water that we humans can detect, and that whether it's the water pulling the stick down or our own sense, deep in our guts, pushing the stick toward water, we'll never really know." Mr. Jasper pats the Y. "But this stick has found me water before, so I say there's something to it."

It makes me think about Ms. Leavitt and her gobbledygook feelings and how if Mr. Jasper is right, we humans carry a lot in our guts.

Mr. Jasper hands us little paper cups that he brought from his science lab and shows us how to dig around the bubbling water and fill our cup, and I'm not even upset that we didn't find a tin bin full of candy because this water tastes so good. Maybe because we found it ourselves, or maybe because I was expecting it to taste all muddy and mossy and instead it tastes clean and clear.

On our way back to school, we pause on the top of

the hill and look back over the valley toward where we found the spring. "See how lush it is? How green? There are clues everywhere," he says. "The earth is telling us all we need to know. We just have to listen."

When we get back to the gazebo I look for Oliver so I can tell him that we found scat in the woods, and that Mr. Jasper and his Y-shaped stick have some kind of sixth sense, but most of the Sports Club kids have left and Oliver's bike is gone from the rack.

I think maybe the water from that spring had special energy boosters or something because I decide I'm going to ride fast to Oliver's street, even though it's kind of far and mostly uphill. But I want to tell him how maybe I can find magic water bubbling up from the earth when we go on the Appalachian Trail this summer, and how we need to start searching for Y-shaped sticks to fasten to our packs.

It's getting cold, and I try to pull my sweatshirt sleeves down over my hands as I ride. I pedal as fast as I can right past the bookstore, and I'm hoping Mom's not looking out the window at that exact moment, and I hope that spring water really did give me super-speed-boosters so I'm not too late when I ride back to meet her and have to hear a whole speech about how I'm not acting responsibly.

I stand up on my pedals until my legs burn, and now I'm hot and pushing the sleeves of my sweatshirt up past my elbows, and when I get to the top of the hill and turn onto his street, I can see him riding, but he's far ahead and I'm too winded to shout.

When he gets to his yard he drops his bike and picks up the ball in the driveway, and when I get closer I see something I haven't seen before, because I haven't been to Oliver's house forever. At first, I think it's one of those political yard signs stuck in the grass, but it's not. It's not that kind of sign at all.

It's a sign that says FOR SALE.

With a picture of that lady, Ms. Myers's friend from math class.

The real estate agent.

I slow down and stop so Oliver can't see me and pull my bike over toward the shrubs on the other side of the street, and when he starts dribbling I pull my whole bike and my whole self into the bushes like we're six and playing hide-and-go-seek. The branches are scratching up my arms, and one goes right up my nose, and I'm not even sure why I'm hiding.

I just watch. I watch as he dribbles the ball a couple of times and starts shooting, basket after basket, on the old hoop where his dad used to practice when we were little.

My brain is telling my body to move, to drag my bike out from these shrubs and go ask my friend what's going on. And I keep saying I will, after the next shot. After the next basket I'll walk over there, and put my hands out, and ask him to pass me the ball, and ask him if he's really moving, and where, and why he didn't tell me, and then I'll shoot a terrible air ball, and make him laugh, and say that we'll be best friends forever no matter what.

But I just keep watching him through the branches.

He misses the next shot, and when he catches the rebound he draws his arm behind his head and hurls the ball one hundred miles per hour at the backboard. It hits with a *bam*, and he lets it fly back through the air and roll into the yard. Then I see his shoulders kind of collapse a little, and he sniffs and wipes his face with his sweatshirt.

I wonder, for a minute, if this is what Reuben is doing at recess. Really watching us, not just looking around but studying our faces and feeling what we're feeling. Not like a spy, but like a regular kid who is good at listening. Like how Vera and Rae could smell and hear the change in the woods today, and how Mr. Jasper can feel the energy of the water in the earth. Because I can hear Oliver's sadness right now, and I know I should roll out of this shrub and go to him.

Then my phone vibrates in my pocket, and I'm sure my mom has called out a search team and soon they'll find me here, in the bushes, across the street from my best friend's house, with a big thought bubble floating up from my head wondering what is going on and how I can help.

Oliver wipes his eyes with the sleeve of his sweatshirt again and starts into his garage, and even though I want to call out to him, I just watch him scoop up his book bag, open his door, and close it behind him.

And I know what Rae would call me. A baby. And she'd be right.

20.

OVER CORN POPS THE next morning, Dad tells me that Rosalie's passing was peaceful, and that even on her last day she was giving him *h-e-l-l*, telling him that someone needs to get that woman in the next bed over watermelon Jell-O because she hates the lime.

"She was the real deal," I say.

Dad reaches out and pats my hand with his hero-hand. "Just like you."

I want that to be true.

Oliver's bike is already in the rack when I get to school the next morning. I park mine next to his and head in through the double doors. He's not in the lobby, or at his locker, or in Ms. Leavitt's room. I check the cafeteria, too, and I don't know why I'm spending all this time looking because I know exactly where he is. Maybe I'm just not sure what I'll say yet.

I take a deep breath and open the gym door. Oliver is going up for a shot and I startle him and he misses, and when he grabs the rebound he slams the ball hard.

"What are you doing here?" he says.

"I was looking for you because I—we found scat in the woods during Nature Club."

"What?" he says. "What's scat?"

"Little rolly pebbles of animal poop!"

He laughs a little but it feels fake, and he starts to tell me how he really just wants to get some court time in before Principal Tacker comes and makes him leave, and I'm wondering why he has to practice so much since he always wins three-on-three at recess no matter who his teammates are. He could probably even win if I were on his team.

He turns to take another shot, and I take a deep breath and think of Rosalie and how she wouldn't be afraid to talk to her own best friend, even if it was about something hard. "I went to your house yesterday," I say. The ball sails through the air, bounces off the rim, and rolls away from the court.

"Sorry," I say. And I'm not even sure if I'm saying sorry about the shot, or for hiding in his bushes, or the fact that there's a FOR SALE sign sticking out of his yard.

The bell rings and he says, "Let's go." Then he picks up his book bag and walks after his basketball and out the gym door.

I keep right up with him and say, "I was riding over to tell you about the scat, but then, well, I thought my mom would get worried because I was late to meet her at the bookstore. I was going to say something, but I had to go. But I saw. . . ."

I feel like such a wuss.

Then he stops and looks right at me and pulls on the straps of his book bag. "Yeah," he says. "We're moving."

I have a hundred questions, like *Why?* and *Where?* and *Are you sure?* and *Will we still have our backpacking trip?* but all that comes out is, "Oh." And my heart feels like it drops into my guts, and my eyes are burning.

We're both watching our shoes as we walk. "It's been kind of hard for my mom," he says. "You know, since . . ." I nod. Since his dad left.

"Layla's in college, and that costs a lot. And Shawna and Rebecca are already talking about going too," he says. Then he bounces the ball hard, even though we're not allowed to bounce balls in the hallways. "My mom said it was time to sell the house."

"Oh," I say.

"But we're trying to find a place to stay in town. Just . . . a smaller place."

"Oh," I say.

"It's no big deal," he says, and stops for a drink at the water fountain. I'm thinking about that whole office room at Knox and Kobe's house, how Oliver wanted to carry it away, make it a home. I'm thinking about the big numbers in math class, down payments, and twenty percent, and all that interest that was too confusing for me to calculate so I left those problems blank. And I'm thinking about the stairs down to Oliver's basement and how we used to fly over them on cardboard sleds when we were little. And I'm thinking it sounds like a big deal.

I wait for him to finish his slow drinks, and we walk on to Ms. Leavitt's room, and the whole time I'm thinking of a hundred things I could have said that would have been better than *Oh*.

Reuben is reading Rae's first letter when we get to class. He's smiling and pointing to different parts and giving her a high five.

Oliver and I sit at our table, and I'm trying to think of something to make him feel better, so I say, "At least we know another word for poop."

And it works. It makes him laugh, and not even a fake one. "That's true," he says. But I can tell neither of us really feels any better.

Ms. Leavitt tells us to take out our notebooks for *Moment of Meditation* and starts the clock. Everyone begins right away. Some kids are using it to work on their projects, which is fine since Ms. Leavitt says there are no rules to *Moment of Meditation*. Chaz has that box full of papers on his table again, and a roll of string. He starts cutting the paper and making little piles.

I turn to Oliver to see if he wants to look at the sketches I made for the next part of *Gabiver*, but he's looking at his phone in his lap.

"Who's winning?" I whisper.

He glances up for a second and says, "What?"

"Are you looking at the scores?"

"Oh," he says. "Yeah, Cavaliers won last night. Lakers too." Then he turns off his phone and slides it in his book bag.

I see Rae pulling something from her book bag. It's her project from last year, black-and-white copies of photographs of her grandma that she transformed with colored pencils and Sharpies into cool, modern-looking self-portraits. I remember her telling Reuben about them before, and I wish I were sitting closer so I could see better. Reuben points to something in one of the portraits, and Rae smiles and nods.

I tap my pencil on my notebook and try out another

one of those down-the-page poems. I'm thinking about Oliver and how I want to tell him that I'm sorry, and that I bet it feels scary and terrible, and that I'll always be his best friend. And I want to tell him that I know his mom seems stressed because I saw her in the office when she said *damn* to Principal Tacker.

So I write:

Sometimes
Crap
Attacks your
Teammate

I'm about to share the poem with Oliver when I hear whispering and laughing. I look back, and Chaz and Saunders are covering their mouths, their shoulders shaking with giggles. I can already feel gobbledygook in my guts, and I don't even know what they're laughing at. Reuben slams his notebook shut and stares back at them.

Ms. Leavitt is making her way to the back of the room when I hear Chaz whisper, "Rabid Reuben. His mom won't even leave him alone with his own brothers."

"Seriously, what's your problem?" Rae says.

Ms. Leavitt signals for Chaz and Saunders and Rae to get up. On the way out of the classroom, Chaz mumbles, "Let your boyfriend speak for himself," and Rae gives him a shove, and he stumbles a step, and he deserves it.

Then the door closes. And I glance over to Reuben, and he's got a look that reminds me of Ms. Leavitt's. A *Who are you?* look.

I nudge Oliver's elbow. "Did you tell them anything?"

"They asked me if we saw Reuben there again," Oliver says. "What was I supposed to do? Lie?" He looks at me. "I just said yes and that he's the twins' brother. It's not a big deal."

I don't know what to say, because he's sort of right; we *did* see Reuben there again, but now everyone thinks he's even weirder than they thought before, and I know in my guts that it *is* a big deal, and Reuben's looking right at me like I better fix this.

And I know I should stand up and tell everyone that Reuben isn't rabid or roaming or rude, that Knox and Kobe love Reuben, that they hugged painted handprints around him, and that Reuben saved our butts by cleaning stains off the wall that we were only making worse.

And I try. At least, I think I try, but it gets all caught up in my throat and my heart beats so loud it drowns out the whole room and my eyes are blurry and I think I might puke. So I look away and ignore everyone laughing.

And it feels like taking one more tiny step in the wrong direction, and before you know it, your compass arrow is all out of whack and you've lost your way.

I can hear Ms. Leavitt's voice outside the classroom and Rae's, but I can't tell what they're saying. Something, at least.

Oliver slides our comics out from the folder. "Come on," he says. "Chaz and them are the jerks, not us. We didn't do anything." He nudges my elbow. "Let's work on *Gabiver*." I nod and keep my head down and look at all the frames for our story from the day we met, how he encouraged me on the teeter-totter, balanced me, made me feel free. And what's a teeter without a totter?

Then I reach into my bag for my notebook so I can show Oliver my sketch for the big collision scene, but I find the note from yesterday.

Ms. Leavitt thinks if I sit with people, I'll make friends. It doesn't work.

It might.

I smoosh it into a little ball and stick it back in my bag. Way in the bottom.

Then I pull out my English folder. Oliver looks at my sketch and says, "This is perfect." He grabs a black colored pencil to start a final draft, and I'm watching him draw his left side, sewed up to my right. His curly hair and basketball jersey and high-top shoe connected to my straight hair, one glasses lens, and T-shirt. And I'm wondering how you can be so close to someone, stitched-up, best-friends close, and not know what's in their guts.

His face right now looks the same as in that first frame on the teeter-totter, sad.

I pat his nondrawing hand, the one holding the paper steady, and say, "I wish you felt like you could have told me," I whisper. "About moving."

"It's no big deal," he says, and keeps drawing. "I'm sure we'll find a place to rent for a while until my mom can make a little more money."

The pages for our comic are spread out on the table, and I keep looking back to that first one.

"It *is* a big deal," I say.

He blows away some eraser dust from the paper and keeps working. "Yeah," he says. "I guess it is."

He doesn't look up, but it feels different. It feels like the truth.

I slide him my *SCAT* poem.

Sometimes
Crap
Attacks your
Teammate

He smiles and his eyes get all teary, but he blinks fast, then reaches over and doodles a pile of poop chasing a stick-figure-Oliver down the street.

"I'm sorry for all your crap," I tell him. "But I'm pretty sure we can get through any scat, or guano, or dirty diapers, together. I mean, we're Gabiver and all."

He nods, and we continue to work on our comic until Ms. Leavitt comes back in with Rae and Saunders and Chaz. Chaz goes back to his table and mumbles something to Orin. Then I peek back at him and watch him work. He's still cutting the strips of paper, hole-punching, and tying strings, fastening them to the roof of his box. For every other project ever, Chaz has written fancy essays that are three pages longer than the assignment and proofread by his mom, so it feels weird to see him working on a kidlike diorama made from a shoebox that he doesn't even work on extra at home.

I'm finishing up the final colors and speech bubbles for the big collision scene in our comic while Oliver starts thinking about the next scene, the one where together, as Gabiver, we will solve some crime.

I look back at Reuben and give him the same wave to see if he'll join us again. Maybe I can explain that we weren't trying to spread any rumors, and that Chaz Gilbertson hasn't shut his mouth since kindergarten, and that I liked when he joined our group last time. But

Reuben shakes his head like *No way.*

I want to push that out of my mind, so I turn back to Oliver. "Can you think of any crimes for Gabiver?"

He taps his pencil on the table. "Maybe someone's stealing all the chocolate milk from the lunchroom?" I shrug. "Or," he says, "maybe Gabiver takes back all the cell phones from Ms. Tacker's desk and returns them to their rightful owners?"

"That one's not bad," I say.

Then Rae passes by our table on her way to the pencil sharpener and gives us a good glare. "Way to go opening your big mouths and letting everyone go on thinking what they want to think when you know it's a load of baloney sandwiches," she says. "What happened to leave no trace?"

I shift in my seat.

"We didn't do anything," Oliver mumbles.

"Exactly," Rae says.

21.

OLIVER AGREES THAT WE shouldn't be even one minute early to Knox and Kobe's, so after school we sit on the swings and share my string cheese sticks.

"No painting today," I tell him.

He laughs and nods. "Then maybe Reuben won't come down," he says.

I know I'm supposed to say *Yeah*, but instead I say, "I don't really mind if he does."

Oliver peels a string from the cheese and says, "Yeah, I guess."

We wait until all the buses leave the circle, then get our bikes from the rack and ride to their house. It's exactly three thirty when we pull into their driveway.

Paula answers the door and walks us to the kitchen,

where Knox and Kobe are sitting at the counter eating sliced grapes. "Gabe! Oyiver!" they say.

"We paint?" one of them asks. I check his left pointer finger.

"I don't think so today, Kobe," I say.

Paula gives a little smile, and I wonder if she knows about our paint-up-the-wall fiasco and how Reuben had to come rescue us with a spray bottle and sponge.

"Pyease?" they say together.

"We'll see," Oliver says.

I shoot him a look like *What the heck? We are definitely not painting.*

Then Paula grabs a baking dish covered in foil from the counter and says, "I have to deliver this to a neighbor down the street. It'll just be five minutes. Will you all be OK?"

We nod, but really I'm thinking, *No! Don't go! There are a thousand things that could go wrong!* But Oliver looks calm and says, "We'll be fine, right, guys?"

Knox and Kobe scream with excitement, and Paula says, "I'll be four houses down on the left. If you need something, holler. Literally." Then she slides into her clogs and rushes out the door to the garage.

"More gwapes," Knox says.

But I think I remember hearing that grapes are the number one choking food for toddlers, and my mom basically just stopped slicing them for me, so I try to divert their attention to Bunny, who's lying facedown on the counter.

"How's Bunny doing?" I ask.

"Bunny OK. I check his ear," Knox says.

We lift them down from the counter, and they both grab an ear of the bunny and pull, and it becomes a tug-of-war. "I check!" Kobe shouts.

"No, me!" says Knox.

I'm wondering if Reuben is upstairs and can hear us flailing, and I'm wishing they would just drop the bunny and the yelling because I don't want him to have to come rescue us again with some magical potion to end bunny-ear tugs-of-war.

"Want to see a cool comic we're making?" I grab my book bag and take out our English folder. Knox and Kobe drop the bunny and run over.

We sit on the floor in the playroom and show them the last drawing we finished, the one where Oliver and I are sewn into Gabiver. I'm explaining to them that Gabiver is half me and half Oliver.

"See?" I say, and point to Oliver's curly hair and then to the drawing. "And see?" I say tugging on my own hair and pointing to Gabiver's right side.

Knox and Kobe giggle and say, "Draw us!"

Oliver laughs and says, "The two of you stitched

together would look just like one of you. You're identical twins!"

"No! I yike purple," Knox says. "Kobe yike green. We different."

Oliver says OK and grabs a piece of their art paper and a pencil from his book bag. "Let's see what I can do." He starts sketching. Knox and Kobe crowd in around him and giggle.

"Which me?" Knox says.

Oliver finds purple and green crayons from their art supplies and colors in half of the character's T-shirt purple and the other half green. He colors light brown curls for hair and even has the left hand turned out with a tiny brown freckle in the crease behind the knuckle. "Me!" says Kobe.

Oliver slides it over to me for a speech bubble, and I write, *Together we're . . . Knobe!*

They giggle and point and say, "We keep it?"

"Sure," I say. Then Paula comes back in through the garage door, and they run to show her the drawing.

"It us!" they giggle.

"That's wonderful," she says. Then she turns to us. "I hear you ran into Reuben here the other day. Has he shown you any of his drawings?" Oliver and I shake our heads. "You should ask him sometime. He's pretty darn impressive, that kid." Then she kisses Knox and Kobe on the tops of their heads. "Not much for babysitting," she says. "But quite the artist." Then she puts her earbuds in and heads down to the basement.

Kobe looks at Oliver's drawing again and says, "Bruvver make us pictures too."

And before I can think of what to say they're both standing at the bottom of the stairs shouting for Reuben.

"Oh, it's OK, he doesn't have to . . ." Oliver starts, but Reuben is already standing at the top of the stairs, looking down.

"Gabe and Oyiver draw!" Kobe says. He waves the drawing over his head.

"Oh, Reuben knows," I say. "He's seen our drawings in school."

"Come see!" Kobe says, and reaches out his hand.

Reuben looks down at me. I shrug and look up at him, and I hope I'm sending him a message with my face that says, *I'm sorry, and I'm so full of gobbledygook, and I hope you come down.*

I know he's still mad, but Knox and Kobe are shouting for him, so he gives me one good look that says, *I'm coming down, but it's not for you.* Then he walks down the stairs and unlocks the baby gate at the bottom.

He takes the drawing from Kobe, and his eyes get *Wow*-big. He points to the tiny freckle behind the left pointer finger knuckle and snorts a laugh and points to Kobe.

"Me!" Kobe says, then points to the other side. "That Knox."

Then I step toward him and say, "It's half Kobe, half Knox. See?"

Reuben traces his finger down the stitches in the middle of the drawing, separating the green half of the shirt from the purple.

"Knobe," I say. "It's kind of like the comic we're working on in school." Reuben nods.

"The idea comes from this graphic novel," Oliver adds. "You've probably never heard of it."

Then Reuben rolls his eyes and nods his head up the stairs, telling us to follow him. Knox and Kobe go up first, and they have to hike their legs up high for each step.

I look at Oliver. "Aren't we supposed to keep them down here?" I whisper.

"Come!" Knox says. Then he turns around on the stairs and waves us up, but Reuben grabs his hand quickly and puts it back on the railing. Then he bends right down to look in Knox's eyes and points to his little hand on the railing.

"I know," Knox says. "Hold tight."

This is really making me wonder why Reuben isn't watching his own brothers. He seems way better at it than we are, but when I look up at him, he's taking a deep breath like Knox lifting his hand from the railing for that one millisecond really jumbled up his insides and he has to blow away all that worry. He's worse than my mom.

We follow him upstairs into his bedroom, and almost every inch of his walls is covered with posters of basketball players and superheroes, and there's a bulletin board hanging next to his dresser that's cluttered with a hundred drawings.

"You like LeBron James?" Oliver asks, and Reuben looks at him like *Duh*, and they both laugh, and I kind of feel like I'm on the outside of some cool-points basketball connection.

Then Reuben gestures to his bookshelves, and I count along the spines. He has all the *Dog Man*s, even the newest one. He also has all the *Diary of a Wimpy Kid*s, and everything by Raina Telgemeier, *New Kid* and *Class Act*, *Twins*, and *When Stars Are Scattered*. Plus a whole shelf of comic books.

"Cool," I say. "If you like *When Stars Are Scattered*, you might like *All Thirteen*. It's not a graphic novel, but it's the kind of true story that keeps you up all night. I loved it."

Then Oliver looks up and does that *Me too* sign.

Reuben nods and laughs and points to his bed, which is unmade and has tons of pillows. There's a library copy of *All Thirteen* tossed on the comforter with one of those bookmark-lights clipped to the cover.

I smile, and Reuben looks at me with huge eyes, and I know what he's saying. He's saying, *I can't believe they've been trapped in that cave for so long, and I know they all get out, but seriously, how?*

"I have that same light," I say. Reuben smiles.

Knox and Kobe grab our hands. They want us to see their room, and they yank us toward the door, but I stop in front of Reuben's bulletin board. He has a bunch of doodles from the back of the Dog Man books where the author shows you all the steps for drawing the characters, but he also has some comics with characters I've never seen before and full-size portraits of Kobe and Knox.

"You're good at drawing people," Oliver says.

Reuben nods.

Kobe yanks on my hand again, and when we're in the hallway on the way to their room, I say, "I saw the one of Rae downstairs on your refrigerator."

He rolls his eyes and sighs, and I can tell exactly what he's saying: *My mom put it there, and she's a little over the top.* I know a thing or two about that. And I wonder if he was the one that hung Knox and Kobe's scribbles over it.

"Who?" Kobe asks, pulling me through the door to their bedroom.

"She's a girl in our class," I say.

"The yistener," Kobe says, and Reuben nods like they've had a hundred conversations about her over dinner.

Knox and Kobe's room is messier than Reuben's. There are these giant Lego-type blocks scattered on the floor, a dollhouse with all the furniture spilled out, and a few puzzle pieces that don't seem to belong anywhere.

"Big-boy beds!" Knox says, and climbs up on a bed with a purple comforter and starts to bounce. Reuben rushes over and carries him off and gets right down on his knees and looks into his eyes.

"I know," Knox says. "No jump."

Then he turns to Oliver and me and says, "He extra caring."

"You mean *careful*?" Oliver asks.

Knox shakes his head. "No, caring."

I nod and say, "I think you're right," and Oliver says we better get back downstairs before Paula finds out we let them up here.

"Come draw!" Kobe says, and pulls Reuben out to the hallway.

"Yeah!" Knox cheers.

Reuben shakes his head and waves them off, but before I know it I'm saying, "You should. It'd be fun."

I look at Oliver and he shrugs and says, "You could help us with the next frame of *Knobe*."

Reuben smiles, and Knox and Kobe squeal, and we all walk down the stairs, Reuben holding tight to his brothers' hands.

We sit on the floor of the playroom with pads of drawing paper laid out and ask Knox and Kobe what their character, Knobe, wants.

"Save the planet from pollution?" I suggest. "Catch a robber?"

They look at each other and say, "Yoyipops!"

Reuben laughs and leans over the paper. He looks at Oliver's first drawing and sketches his own version of Knobe, but this time he makes it look like an X-ray, with a stomach full of lollipops.

We all laugh as Reuben adds lollipop trees and a lollipop sun and a lollipop-wheeled tricycle to the picture.

Knox and Kobe scribble green and purple all over Reuben's perfect lollipops, but he doesn't care. He smiles and shakes his head and puts his arms around his brothers. Oliver draws their house in the background and adds a lollipop picket fence around the yard.

I draw two speech bubbles in the shapes of lollipops

coming from both sides of Knobe's mouth. *We stick together!* says the first one. And the second one says, *LOL(lipop)!*

Reuben laughs and puts his fist out for a bump. I connect my knuckles with his, and Oliver explains to Knox and Kobe what *LOL* means, and *they* start to LOL, rolling around the floor. "Yike this?" Knox says.

Reuben tickles them and starts picking up the colored pencils from the floor. He sees my English folder on the art table where we were showing Knox and Kobe our *Gabiver* comic, and he looks through the drawings.

"Those are the same ones from class," I say.

He nods and pauses on the one with me laughing on the teeter-totter and Oliver looking sad and out toward the parking lot, then he traces around Oliver's face in the drawing and looks up. I think Oliver is going to look away, or say that he still needs to fix that one, but he doesn't. And I count to two-one-thousand, which actually feels like one-thousand-one-thousand, before they look away.

Reuben hands Oliver the drawing, and we hear the basement door open. I check my watch. Five twenty-five. And I can't believe the minutes went by today without me watching them.

"Well," Paula says. "It sure sounds like you all are having a good time."

She's looking through her purse and saying, "And of course I don't have the right change again. . . ." She pulls out a bill for each of us and says, "But who am I kidding? This time is priceless."

I feel weird taking twenty dollars from Reuben's mom when we were kind of all just hanging out this time, but Oliver puts his money right into his pocket, so I take the bill and fold it in half. Then I hold it up between my fingers and say, "We're saving for a backpacking trip."

I look at Oliver and he nods and says, "Yeah."

"What?" Kobe asks.

"We're going hiking and sleeping out in the woods for three nights and four days, and we need fancy backpacks and water-holder things."

"Water-holder things?" Paula asks.

I keep going on and on about the water bladders and how they have tubes that attach to our packs so we can drink whenever we want, and I don't know why I'm blabbing so much, except I guess that I'm still feeling weird about taking the money because today was even pretty fun, and I want her to know that we're using it for something important, and not just one thousand creemees at the country store or something. And I'm looking at Oliver, hoping he'll jump in to talk about how much those magic wicking shirts cost, but he's just kind of looking down at his feet and not saying a thing.

And when I'm talking about hiking thirty-five miles and climbing two peaks, Reuben's eyes get big again. *Wow*-big.

"That sounds fun!" Paula says.

Then Knox comes and wraps himself around my leg. "Be extra caring."

22.

I DON'T REALIZE UNTIL Sunday that Oliver has our English folder with all the *Gabiver* drawings. He must have slid them in his bag after class on Friday, but I want to lay them all out and start thinking about the next part, the part where Gabiver's going to solve a crime.

I send him a text. *Want to work on* Gabiver?

Sure. I'll be over in 20, he writes back.

I'm about to go tell Mom that Oliver's coming over because she likes to know so she can make enough dinner in case he wants to stay. But I stop at my door and send him another message.

Why don't I come there?

He doesn't write back, and I'm wondering if he's already on his bike.

I'll bring string cheese, I add.

A minute later he responds. *OK.*

I pack my book bag with some colored pencils and an art pad, then tap on Puppy's cage and tell her I'll be back later. When I get downstairs Mom is reading on the couch with her feet up on the coffee table.

"I'm going to Oliver's house to work on *Gabiver*," I say.

She looks at me over the rims of her glasses.

"*May* I go to Oliver's house to work on *Gabiver*?" I ask. "It's due on Wednesday."

"I assume his mom is home," she says.

I'm not sure if his mom is home or not, but technically she didn't ask. She's just assuming. So I nod at her assumption.

Mom says, "OK" and "Good luck," and I grab a couple of string cheese sticks from the refrigerator and head out the door.

When I get there, Oliver is outside practicing dribbling around a fake defender. I drop my bike in the yard and try not to stare at the FOR SALE sign.

"Want to try that with a real defender?" I ask.

He pretends like he's looking all around, right past me. "I don't see any real defenders." He laughs at his own joke, which makes me laugh, and then he tosses me the ball.

He's right, though. I don't have any moves.

"Just stand here." He points to a spot on his driveway. "And don't let me close to the net. Don't let me jump."

I put my arms out and bounce on my toes like I see the kids do at recess and Sports Club, but Oliver dribbles easily around me and jumps up for a shot. The ball circles the rim but bounces out. Then he grabs it with both hands and slams it to the ground. "Damn!"

"Hey," I say. "It's just a shot."

"It's not just a shot!"

I get the ball from where it rolled off in the yard, and I'm not sure why he's so upset or when he got so competitive. Watching him shoot hoops used to be fun. I'd call "Aaaair baaaaall" or "Nothing but rim!" when he missed, and we'd laugh and laugh. But not anymore.

I toss the ball back to him. "OK, then," I say. "Try again."

This time, he dribbles it around me, sinks it in the basket, and pumps his fist. "There," he says.

"Are you trying out for a team or something?" I ask.

He bounces the ball a couple of times and shoots again. Makes it. "Not really," he says.

I look at him like *What's that supposed to mean?* And he says, "Sorry I got so mad. I just really hate missing."

"It's OK," I say. Then I put my arm around his shoulders. "Let's go in."

There are empty boxes stacked in the corner of the living room, and I'm trying not to look at them, and trying not to imagine Oliver packing all his stuff inside them, and trying not to imagine them stacked in a moving truck to some new place.

It takes me about ten seconds to figure out that his mom is not home. I hand him a string cheese and say, "Where's your mom?"

"She picked up an extra weekend shift." He unwraps the cheese and peels a string. "She'll be home soon," he says.

I'm not supposed to be at anyone's house unless a grown-up is there too. When I asked my mom why, she listed a hundred reasons like *What if there's a fire? What if you choke? What if a stranger knocks on the door?* and even though I know it's perfectly safe here without Oliver's mom, I'm trying to push all those mom-thoughts out of my brain.

I peel a string of cheese and chew it a hundred times before swallowing just to be safe; then we spread out our drawings across the kitchen counter in order.

"Any more ideas on the crime?" I ask.

"Maybe there's an evil referee?" he says. "Who's letting fouls go uncalled. And Gabiver has to stop him."

I nod, thinking.

"Or maybe he has some time-traveling superpowers,

and whatever player he taps can travel back in time to fix a missed shot, or unfoul someone, or just change wherever they went wrong," he says.

I nod. "That would be cool."

"I could use that," he says. "I could really use that."

I'm pretty sure he's talking about basketball, but the look on his face makes me wonder if he's thinking about fixing something other than just a free throw or rebound.

I'm trying to come up with some more ideas, but my eyes keep landing back on that same drawing. I pull it toward me and trace my finger around Oliver's body on the teeter-totter like Reuben did.

"You still look sad in this one," I say.

Oliver rolls the colored pencil between his fingers for a few seconds. He doesn't look up when he says, "My dad was supposed to pick me up that day." He keeps rolling the pencil between his fingers. "I was worried he would be late and then my mom would be mad. And then I was worried that he forgot about me and left." The colored pencil drops to the floor. "He definitely forgot about me that day, but it took him a bunch more years to leave."

He's still looking down, so I pick up the colored pencil from the floor and move a little closer, until our shoulders touch, and I look at his face in the drawing instead.

"I'm sorry."

"It's not a big . . ."

But before he can finish, I hand him the colored pencil and pat his hand, the way my dad pats my hand after Corn Pops, and I'm hoping a little bit of his hero rubs off me and onto Oliver, and I hope it makes him feel more comfortable. "It is," I say. "It is a big deal. And it's guano. But if you want to unload it, I'm here."

"Unload my guano on you?" he says.

"Well," I say. "You can't hold it in forever. I'm pretty sure that's bad for you."

We both start laughing and actual, real tears are falling off our chins and landing on our pages. They're not the laughing-so-hard-you-cry tears, but the kind of tears that have been waiting to spill and a little laugh gave them the permission to go. Escape-tears that just needed a nudge to fall.

When we finally quit laughing, I notice he's darkening the lines on the last comic, the big collision scene where the nurse has stitched us into Gabiver.

"Really, though," I say. "I'm here."

He nods and keeps pressing down to darken the lines. "My mom always says that my dad was so happy when she was pregnant with me. He was finally getting a boy. I think she's trying to make me feel like it's obviously not my fault that my dad left, because I was something he was so excited for." Oliver finishes darkening the lines of Gabiver's shoes and begins tracing over the black stitches that connect us down our middle, making them thicker. "But it makes me feel worse. Like maybe I wasn't the right kind of boy."

"Right kind of boy?" I ask.

"I don't know," he says. "Someone who cared more about basketball. Someone who wanted to practice in the driveway."

He presses his pencil down over the basketball in Gabiver's left hand. "When he left I joined a zillion sports and quit wearing my sisters' hand-me-downs, thinking he'd come back."

And now I'm looking at all the frames of our *Gabiver* comic and seeing a different story there. Oliver's story. A worried kid in his sisters' pink fleece and light-up sparkle sneakers, waiting for his dad. And I can't believe I was sitting on the other side of the teeter-totter and had no idea, and I'm thinking that you can't tell who someone is just by their speech bubbles. They're carrying things in their guts.

"You're not the wrong kind of boy," I tell him. "No one is."

He nods. "Well, maybe Chaz."

I chuckle with him because I think he might be right, but now I'm wondering if there's anything in Chaz's guts.

Then the door to the garage opens, and his mom

comes in with canvas grocery bags over her arms, and Oliver gets up fast to help her. When she sees me she says, "Oh, Gabe! Hi!"

I smile and say, "Hi," and shoot a quick text to my mom.

Don't worry, his mom is home.

We help her unpack the groceries, and it doesn't even feel like I haven't been here in forever; it feels normal and good. Even when his mom mentions the FOR SALE sign in their yard, it feels OK because she says, "I'm trying my best to find a place here so you two can stay together."

And Oliver says, "What's a teeter without a totter?"

His mom smiles, and when all the groceries are put away, she sits down with us for a few minutes and asks about the comic.

Oliver looks at me and I look at him. "Well," I say. "It's about these two friends," and I point to the page where Oliver's on the teeter-totter and I'm standing off to the side with a sandbox truck in my hand. "And one of them teaches the other how to teeter-totter, and in the beginning it doesn't go so well. But the first friend doesn't let the other one quit, and after a while they get the hang of it, and now they've been balancing each other out forever."

I think that makes his mom almost-cry because her voice is a little shaky when she points to the big collision scene and asks, "What's happening here?"

"That's where the two friends get in a big accident, and they each damage half their body. Luckily, it's the opposite halves and they can be saved by getting stitched together to become this amazing new superperson."

"Wow," she says.

"You haven't read Dog Man?" I ask.

"Is that what those books are about?" she says, and puts her arm around Oliver's shoulders.

We all laugh.

"Hey," I say. "You know what else these friends used to do?" I point to our comic.

"What?" his mom asks.

I look at Oliver and smile. "They used to slide down the basement stairs in cardboard boxes."

His mom laughs and looks up at the ceiling like she's remembering, and she has those escape-tears in her eyes too. Then she gets up and opens the door to the basement wide.

Oliver looks at her. "Really?" he says.

She nods. "Before I change my mind."

I smile and hop down from the stool to grab one of the moving boxes from the living room. His mom is still standing at the top of the basement stairs, looking down, and I set the box right next to her.

"It's pretty steep," she says. "I can't believe I used to let you kids do this."

"The key is in the cushions," I tell her.

Oliver and I run downstairs and take the big cushions off the couch and line them up along the wall at the bottom of the stairs. We make sure they're balanced, then head back up, right past his mom and out to the garage.

She laughs when we come back inside with our bike helmets on.

"Don't go putting a hole in that wall," she says. "I am trying to sell this house, remember."

"I can't make any promises," I say. And it's a joke, but suddenly I wonder if I *do* put my helmet through their basement wall, if no one will buy the house and they'll have to stay forever.

We clip the straps under our chins and position the box so it's just peeking out over the top step.

"Think we'll both still fit?" I ask.

"Won't know until we try," he says.

I climb in the back and pull my knees to my chest, and Oliver gets in front. It's a tight squeeze and the sides are bulging a little, but we're in.

Oliver pretends to start the engine. "Vroom, vroom!" He scooches the box forward, and I wrap my arms around his shoulders tight, and before I know it we're flying, or bumping, and sliding, and bumping, and flying, and laughing down the stairs and into the couch cushions at the bottom.

His mom is cheering and laughing from the top, and the box has split open along the sides, and we're in a heap with the cushions at the bottom of the stairs.

My eyes are full of those tears, so I laugh hard and let them out, and Oliver says, "One more run?"

I nod, and we take our broken box and do it again, this time holding up the sides as we fly.

After our fifth run, when the box is tattered and worn, I feel a buzz in my pocket, and I know it's time to go.

"I should be getting home," I say.

We drag the cardboard up the stairs, and Oliver unclips his helmet. "Sure you don't want to stay for the game?" he asks, and ducks into the living room to turn on the TV. A commercial comes on loud, and he turns it down. "I could teach you all the positions and rules."

"I know all the positions and rules," I say. But really, I'm a little hazy on "traveling" and how the referees can catch it so quickly.

"Sure you do," he says, and smiles.

My phone buzzes again, and I text my mom that I'm on my way.

I say goodbye to Oliver and his mom and go outside to grab my bike, and as I'm coasting down his street it hits me.

Oliver's been telling me his TV is broken.

23.

MS. LEAVITT GIVES US the whole period to work on our projects, and Oliver tells me to wait a minute, that he has to do something quickly. He borrows a laptop from Ms. Leavitt's cart and keeps his screen so low it looks like the less-than sign in math class. "Our internet is slow at home, and we don't have a printer," he says.

"Are you printing off the scores?" I ask.

He's looking down in his lap and punching numbers into the laptop.

"It seemed like your TV was fixed."

He looks up and says, "Oh, yeah, no, this is different." He points to the laptop but doesn't raise the screen. "It's something for my mom. It's kind of a surprise."

He slides his hands into the keyboard, slouches down to look in, presses a couple of buttons, then closes it and heads to the back of the room.

Rae is walking back from the printer, holding papers, and I reach out and tap her arm. "Hey," I say. "I have something for Vera."

I dig in my book bag and pull out the next two graphic novels in the Real Friends series. "She can return them to me whenever," I say.

Rae smiles and takes the books. "I'll give them to her at lunch." Then she shows me the papers she's holding. "I'll be out of here soon."

"You typed your non-apology letters?" I say. "That's official."

"It is," she says. "I'm very officially not sorry. And I very officially have a lot to say about each incident." I smile and imagine all the not-bad words she used to share her side of the story.

The printer in the back of the room spits out two pages for Oliver, then starts beeping.

"That means the paper drawer is empty," Ms. Leavitt calls. "I can refill it."

Oliver checks the papers in his hands. "This is all I need," he says. Then he folds them and puts them in his pocket.

Rae waves her letters in the air toward Ms. Leavitt

and says, "I wrote the letters. Can I go back to seventh grade now?"

Ms. Leavitt picks up her classroom phone and says she'll call down to the office and check in with Principal Tacker. I know Rae probably wants to be with her friends back in seventh grade, but I got kind of used to her being in our class. I'm secretly hoping that Principal Tacker will read the notes, realize Rae didn't actually apologize, and send her right back to our class, where she can sit next to Reuben and not let kids get away with whispering and laughing along behind anyone's back.

And I'm wondering if maybe I can be brave enough to do that when she's gone.

Rae sits down next to Reuben to wait for Principal Tacker, and Oliver sits back down next to me.

"What's the secret?" I ask him. "For your mom."

"Oh," he says. "Just something I've been working on." He puts his hand over the pocket holding the printed papers. "I'm not even sure it'll work yet."

I'm guessing a hundred guesses in my head. Maybe he found an apartment in town while he was searching online so they can stay here, or maybe it's an application for a new job with more money.

But then Chaz leans back and sends a paper ball sailing through the air. I watch as it lands short of the recycling bin, and everyone laughs. Chaz doesn't get up to toss it in. He laughs along with everyone like he meant to do that and goes back to working on his project.

"Missing like that is a crime." Saunders laughs.

"And then not picking it up?" Rae says. "Double crime."

Then I look at Oliver. "A crime!" I say.

And we're off brainstorming one hundred miles per hour. "Maybe Gabiver is out on the trail," I say. "And maybe he's got some kind of sixth sense for finding all the trash people leave behind, and he's working on cleaning up."

Oliver nods.

"And maybe he's pretty good at following a path even when it's not marked."

Oliver sits up. "He's like a human compass."

"I even know how to use one of those!" I say, which makes Oliver laugh.

He starts sketching out the woods. Trees and trees and leaning-over trees and fallen-down trees and skinny trees and wide trees and more and more trees, with a slight path cut through. Then he adds Gabiver on the trail.

"Draw a compass on his guts or something," I say, and I start to draft out some speech bubbles in my notebook.

There's a tap on my shoulder, and when I turn

around Rae is standing there. "Excuse me," she says. "But if you're writing about a kid who can use a compass, I think I should probably be helping."

"It's for our comic," I say, and gesture for her to join us.

"Let me see." She walks around to the other side of our table, and I slide our comic frames out of my English folder for her to see.

I look up and gesture for Reuben, and I make my whole face say *Please join us*, and he drags over his chair, and all of a sudden we're all together at our table. Rae's across from us, and Reuben sits down next to me, right at my righty drawing arm.

Chaz is peering over his diorama project at us and snickering something to Saunders about a "double date."

Rae shoots him a look and says, "Like you know a thing about dates."

Saunders laughs, and Chaz elbows him hard to get him to quit it. And then everyone just goes back to working.

Rae rolls her eyes and returns her attention to our *Gabiver* drawings.

I pull the new sketch toward me, the one of Gabiver in the woods, and I draw a sign nailed into one of the trees. Leave No Trace, it says. Rae reaches out for a fist bump, and we all four connect knuckles.

Right then Principal Tacker opens the door and calls, "Rae Hendriks? I believe you have something for me?"

Rae stands up and taps the drawing of Gabiver in the woods. "Remember," she says. "One tiny step, and then another."

Oliver and Reuben look at me funny, and I say, "It's a Nature Club thing."

Rae waves bye and follows Principal Tacker out the door, leaving us three sitting in a row with *Gabiver* spread out across the table.

Reuben tears a page from his notebook and starts writing. Then he slides the paper to the middle so we can all see.

Plastic bag in the trees?

Oliver nods and adds a plastic bag caught on one of the branches, and a plastic water bottle floating in a stream.

"After the trail scene, what should be the last frame?" Oliver asks.

"How about the playground?" I say. "He comes back to be a helper at his own school, spotting messes and trying to help clean them up."

"That's perfect," Oliver says. "Because we met on a playground. That's where Gabiver was born."

But as Oliver starts doing a rough sketch of our school playground with kids running across the bouncy bridge and flying through the air on rings, Reuben pushes his chair a couple of inches back from the table and closes his eyes. It looks like he's scared and trying to get away. I think of him pressed against the bricks of the school building, as far from the playground as possible, watching. Silent.

"Are you OK?" I ask.

Reuben tries to smile and inches his chair back to the table.

I point to the sketch of the playground. "Gabiver will be a helper," I say. "Maybe he can use the compass on his guts for something good, to help kids make a path and not get lost or something."

Reuben nods and writes: *Like a therapist.*

I laugh and say, "Probably not *that* good. But maybe like a friend."

That makes Reuben actually smile. And at first Oliver glances down to his shoes, but then he reaches over and taps the word *therapist* and raises his eyebrows into a question.

Reuben nods and looks down, too, but then Oliver taps Reuben's hand and they look at each other for a minute before Oliver makes that *Me too* sign.

"You do?" I ask. "I didn't know. . . ."

He nods and says, "We all went together when my dad left. Then Mom got busy, and my sisters stopped, but I just kind of kept on." He looks down again and rolls the colored pencil between his fingers, and I can't help it but I throw my arm around Oliver's shoulders because I'm thinking that's major cool points, to ask someone to help you wade through all the stuff we carry in our guts.

When Ms. Leavitt says to start packing up our things, Oliver stacks all our comic frames in order, with the last unfinished sketches on the top. Then he puts them all neatly in my English folder.

"You should take them home tonight," I say, handing him the drawings. "So you can finish the last sketches. Then I'll draft the speech and thought bubbles and add them on tomorrow." I start packing up the colored pencils. "And then we'll color them in and be ready for Wednesday," I say.

But Oliver shakes his head and says, "No, you better take it. Just in case." He hands the drawings back to me.

"In case what?"

"I don't know," he says. "In case I forget it or some-thing."

"It's OK," I say, holding out all the frames of our comic. "I trust you."

Oliver exhales a deep breath and puts everything in his English folder and tucks it into his book bag.

In the rest of our classes, we all sit together and work a little on the comics beneath our table. Reuben sits with us in the lunchroom, too, and when I get up for another carton of milk, Chaz spots Oliver and Reuben huddled over the drawings.

He scoffs and laughs and says to Oliver, "Are you guys best friends now?"

I'm on my way back and just close enough to hear him, but before I can say anything Oliver turns around and says, "No." And I'm pretty sure I see him edge just the tiniest inch away from Reuben.

Chaz laughs and says, "Oh I see. He's just buzzing around you like a little clingy bug. Roachy Reuben." Saunders nearly spits out his milk, which makes everyone at their table laugh even harder, and then Reuben stands up and gives Chaz a glare.

"Oooo," Chaz says. "You're really cutting me with that look." He grabs his heart and pretends to stumble backward. But then Reuben takes a step forward, and I can tell he really wants to give Chaz a shove while he's off balance like that, send him sprawling across the gross lunchroom floor. And I wish he would. I wish he'd give him a big shove and send him flying across his table, taking all his friends and his friends' lunches with him.

But I remember Knox's voice. *He extra caring.*

And I know that Reuben won't do it. He won't give Chaz the shove he deserves.

If Rae were here, I know what she'd do. She'd swat

Chaz away and tell him that for someone so advanced and gifted he ought to know that roaches don't even buzz. Then she'd squash his stupid little laughs like a bug beneath her sneaker.

She'd squash Oliver too. Because his "No" caused all this. It caused Chaz's laughs and Saunders's milk spray, which set everyone else off. It caused "Roachy Reuben."

And I'm thinking that's what Mr. Jasper was talking about when he said you have to keep your head up and look three steps out in front of you because if you don't, it's easy to lose your way.

And when you do stray off course, you have to stop and backtrack to the last place you were sure about. And I'm thinking back and back to *What's a teeter without a totter?* and flying down Oliver's basement stairs. I'm thinking about my best friend, and how I know his heart is a steady compass, and he just needs to pick his head up and look three steps out in front of him. He needs to be brave enough to change his path.

We both do.

And I know that if Rae were here, she'd look me right in the eyes and tell me to be the real deal.

Chaz returns to his seat, and Orin nudges him and laughs, and when I get back to our table I don't sit. I stand in front of Oliver and say, "Why'd you let him do that?"

"Do what?" he asks.

"Make fun of Reuben," I say.

"I didn't tell him to make fun of Reuben," he says. He looks over at Chaz's table, and I can see his shoulders drop. "I didn't," he says.

"But you let him."

Oliver is trying to brush me off like it's no big deal. But it is. It is a big deal.

"Come on," I say, and when he doesn't budge, I say it again. "Come on," and gesture for him to get up.

"Where are we going?" he asks, but I just keep motioning for him to get up and walk with me. There's a direct path from our table to Chaz's, and I take a deep breath and start stepping, and I know there's not a map for this or a compass to keep you pointed in the right direction, but my guts are telling me it's the right way. And I've gotten pretty good at listening.

When we get there, Oliver and I stand in front of Chaz, and I can almost feel the stitches zigzagging between us.

We're Gabiver.

"You going to say anything?" Chaz asks. "Or maybe your new friend is rubbing off on you?"

I stay silent and count to five-one-thousand, because it's OK to be quiet and think. Oliver shifts a little next to me, but then he settles his weight back onto both of his basketball sneakers and stands tall.

Then I look Chaz in the eyes and ask, "Why do you make fun of Reuben for not talking?"

"What do you mean?" Chaz says, then he looks around his table and lets out a little laugh.

Oliver inches closer to me, and I can feel our stitches tighten.

And now it's Chaz's turn to be quiet. Everyone at his table is looking at him, and waiting, and he just kind of shrugs like *whatever*. So we stand and wait, and I get to ten-one-thousand before I realize I'm trying to answer the same question. Why have we let it happen? Why have we laughed along?

And I think I know the answer: because it's what we've always done. We've made up stories and names and whispered behind his back and followed each other since before he even got here. We took a tiny step off course, and another tiny step, until we looked up and realized we'd ignored our compass; we'd lost our way.

Reuben walks over and stands next to us on my right side. So now we're standing shoulder to shoulder to shoulder. And even though no one is saying anything I'm imagining there are big fat thought bubbles rising above our heads, full of text, and leaking into the next frame, wondering why we've ever made jokes or laughed along and how we can stop it. And I'm thinking, maybe, if we were quieter like this sometimes, we might be able to listen better. To each other, and to our guts.

Principal Tacker claps her hands to get everyone's attention for dismissal to recess and afternoon classes, and I lean toward Chaz and say, "I think we could probably quit it. Quit making fun."

And I think, right now, this might be the realest-deal version of me.

Chaz doesn't say anything. Neither do Saunders and Orin or any of the other kids in our class. We all just spend a silent moment together before Principal Tacker gestures for our tables to stand up and begin filing out the side door to the playground for recess.

We all do a three-way fist bump, and then Oliver rushes to the basketball court, and Reuben stands against the wall of the school like usual.

And instead of finding a dry patch of ground to sit on, I take a spot right next to Reuben on the wall and look out to see what he sees. The whole playground, every piece of equipment, all the fields, the court, around the whole gazebo, and down the entire line of swings.

I hear the echo of Oliver's dribbling against the bricks behind me: *Bam. Bam. Bam.* And if I lean back like Reuben I can feel the vibrations of it in my chest.

24.

REUBEN

HIS SADNESS IS GROWING. And it's the same as mine. Thinking maybe if you were just different, things wouldn't be the way they are.

Wishing you could go back.

Wishing you could fix it.

25.

WHEN I GET TO school, Oliver's bike isn't parked in the rack, and when the bell rings he still hasn't arrived in the lobby. I wonder if maybe he didn't ride today and he's sneaking in some free throw practice, but when I pull open the heavy doors, the gym is empty.

In class, Ms. Leavitt says we can get right to finalizing our projects. Then she does the attendance, checking off names on her clipboard.

Our projects are due tomorrow, and Oliver has the folder with our *Gabiver* comic, and there's no way we can be ready to share if he doesn't show up with it.

Reuben is sitting at our table now, and we're looking at each other, and I know we both have the same thought bubbles. *Where is he?*

At first I'm wondering if Ms. Leavitt will give us extra time since Oliver isn't here, and then after a few more minutes, I start to get worried, because Oliver is never late, and I'm wondering if someone can move that fast, pack up all the empty boxes in their living room, close the door, and drive off to a new life without saying goodbye to their best friend. But I know Oliver wouldn't do that.

Reuben rolls the jagged edge of his bulletin board paper project between his fingers.

I lean over and see that he has two detailed self-portraits drawn on his paper now, one on each side and both outlined in black Sharpie. Each face has a different expression. One is happy and energetic. The other is sad and scared.

In the middle, a big comic-style lightning bolt separates them.

I check the clock on the classroom wall. He's ten minutes late.

I tap my notebook with my pencil and try to jot a down-the-page poem, but I can't think, so I do what Oliver's been doing lately. I sneak my cell phone out of my book bag and into my lap below my desk.

Reuben nods.

Oliver? Where are you? I type.

Then I wait to feel the buzz of my phone in my hands beneath the table.

Ms. Leavitt reminds us about the gallery walk of projects tomorrow and says, "I'm so excited to see how they all come out."

Cass waves Missy and Tonya into the supply closet to help her make a video of the song she wrote. Ingrid is typing up her short story on one of Ms. Leavitt's laptops from the cart, and Chaz is hanging more shreds of paper from the ceiling of his diorama.

Then my phone vibrates, and I nearly jump to the roof.

I wait until Ms. Leavitt walks by on her way to Andre, who has his hand raised in the back. Then I sneak a look beneath the table and see a message from Oliver. I slide my finger across the screen and read: *The folder is in my locker. You know the combination.*

I nudge Reuben to look, and when he reads it his face gets even more serious and he gestures for me to write back.

Where are you? Are you OK? I type.

I'm fine. Just have to do something for my mom.

I show Reuben the screen, then slide the phone in my pocket, and my brain is spinning one hundred miles per hour, wondering why he'd leave the folder in his locker overnight and how he was supposed to finish the drawings. And now something just feels really, really off, and I'm remembering how he tried to get me to take the folder home, like he knew he'd be gone today. But why wouldn't he just tell me that?

I raise my hand and ask Ms. Leavitt if I can go to the bathroom. She nods, and I head out to Oliver's locker.

The folder is on the top shelf, and as I'm reaching for it, I see a picture on the inside beneath the coat hook, where he usually hangs his Sports Club bag. I pull off the magnet that's holding it there, and I feel like I'm looking in on a secret I'm not supposed to see, but once I start looking I can't put it back.

It's a picture of Oliver with his dad. Oliver's sitting next to him. Oliver from third grade, because he's wearing one of those lollipop rings our teacher used to give out after group problem-solving on Friday afternoons. Oliver with his sisters' hand-me-down polar bear shirt, which was his favorite because when you ran your hands across the sequins their color changed from white to blue. He has a basketball in his lap, and they look like they're on the bleachers at a game. I remember his dad used to take him to college games at the University of Vermont, and the next day he'd tell me about the pretzels that were the size of his face that came with salt as big and shiny as diamonds.

Oliver's smiling. But the picture makes me feel sad.

I return the picture to the inside of his locker, beneath the hook, and tuck the folder under my arm on the way back to Ms. Leavitt's room.

Reuben is bent over his project but lifts his head when I walk in. We open the folder, and everything looks just as we left it, except when I pull out the comic frames the last two drawings are done.

The trail scene is filled out with more shrubs and logs, and the compass on Gabiver's belly is pointing north. He's picking up a piece of trash beneath the Leave No Trace sign.

And in the last scene, kids are playing on the jungle gym, shooting baskets on the court, swinging, climbing, and sliding, and Gabiver is there, in the middle of the playground standing between two kids, one who is pointing and laughing and needs a full speech bubble full of all-caps HA-HAs, and another who is small with eyes facing down. Gabiver's right hand is on the smaller kid's shoulder, like a hero-hand trying to make him feel more comfortable.

Reuben points to the brick of the school wall, and sure enough, there he is. But he's leaning forward, like maybe he's about to take a step.

"It's perfect," I say. "But he came in and dropped it off early? And never said anything?"

Reuben looks at me with worried eyes, and something feels wrong in my guts.

I raise my hand and ask Ms. Leavitt if I can go to my locker for a few supplies. She's loading the printer with more paper, and it automatically starts a print job from the day before. She looks up and says, "OK," and I walk fast to the door, and when I'm in the hall, I run. And I don't care that it's against the rules or that if Principal Tacker catches me, she will point me right into the office and ask me what I think I was doing out there.

I turn down the hallway and don't stop until I'm in the bathroom. I pull out my phone and call Oliver, and it rings and rings. I hang up and try again, but he doesn't pick up.

I text again. *Are you sure you're OK?*

And this time, I don't hear back.

When I open the door I almost run square into Ms. Neely, who's headed toward the gym. "Can I help you?" she asks.

I want to say yes, that I need everyone's help. That I've lost my best friend and I don't know which direction to turn, but I just let the bathroom door slam and run toward the exit doors and look as far as I can down the sidewalk toward town.

The eighth graders are outside on the playground,

climbing and swinging and hanging from the jungle gym.

The basketball court is empty.

And I feel frozen, because I don't know where to look. The recess aide blows her whistle and waves down two kids racing up the slide.

"It's OK," I whisper to myself. "I'll find him."

Then I take one step, and another, back into school.

26.

REUBEN

I SHOULDN'T BE RUNNING in the hall. I shouldn't be running at all.

The kid who slipped on that thin layer of ice was running.

Then he flew. Over the rail. Popping all my speech bubbles on his way down. His head sending a ringing sound up the metal pole.

That sound still rings in my ears.

If I had been quiet, not pulling at the recess teacher's jacket to listen to my story. Then maybe she would have seen him, blown her whistle. Told him to stop running. Maybe she would have caught him or cushioned his fall.

Maybe he'd still be here.

Instead of that ringing in my ears.

Maybe the best thing I can be is quiet and still.

Except now.

Now I need to be quiet and *running* because we have to find Oliver. And I think I have a clue.

So I run.

I run from Ms. Leavitt's room down the hall with the paper in my hand.

27.

WHEN I GET BACK inside the school, I see Reuben running toward me with a piece of paper in his hand.

It has a printed picture of a dog sprinting across the top of the page with the word *Greyhound* beneath. And there's a confirmation number, and a price, and I know exactly what this is. It's a receipt for a bus ticket. To somewhere in Massachusetts. Reuben looks at me with his eyebrows all scrunched up.

"His dad," I say. "Did you find this in his folder?"

Reuben shakes his head.

"The classroom?" He nods and gestures his hand like the paper's coming out of the printer.

"When Ms. Leavitt loaded the printer," I say. "This page came out?" I read the receipt again. "It's got to be

Oliver's. He was the last person to use it yesterday before it ran out of paper and beeped."

Reuben's still looking at me with scrunched-up eyebrows.

"But he doesn't visit his dad," I say. "He never has. He left two years ago, and Oliver hasn't seen him since . . . I don't even know when." I look at the paper again. "And he would have told me if he were going. Right?"

My eyes feel all burny, and I look down at my feet.

"He thinks it's his fault. That his dad left."

Reuben lets go of a big, heavy breath.

"I'll call his mom," I say. I take out my phone, right there in the hallway, without even trying to hide it, first to look up the restaurant where she works in town, then to call. But the line is busy. I hang up and try again.

Reuben points to the ticket. The bus leaves in forty minutes.

I slide my phone back in my pocket, and even though I know I'm going to get in trouble— Ms. Leavitt will tell Principal Tacker, and Principal Tacker will call my mom at the bookstore, and as soon as she finds me she'll ban me from everything in the world—I run out the front door of the school, hop on my bike, and pedal up the sidewalk toward town.

And I can hear Reuben pedaling right there behind me all the way to the restaurant because it's so obvious to me now that Reuben is the real deal. He always has been.

When we pass by the bookstore I don't check to see if Mom's in the window, watching me skip out on school and ride like the wind through town, because even if she comes out on the porch waving her arms with boxes of all my favorite books, signed by the author, with fancy matching bookmarks, she can't stop me.

We ditch our bikes in front of the restaurant, and a bell on the door jingles when we walk in. I see Oliver's mom right away, taking an order at the counter. When she hears the bell chime she looks up.

"Gabe?"

I hold up the Greyhound bus receipt and say, "Can I talk to you for a second?"

She tells the man at the counter to excuse her for just a moment and gestures for us to go outside.

"What's going on, Gabe?" she asks.

I explain to her that Oliver hasn't shown up for school today, that we found this in Ms. Leavitt's printer, and we think it's his, and that he finished his part of our group project and left it for us in his locker this morning.

She reaches for the paper, and her face sinks, and she says one word very loudly.

"Damn."

Then she stuffs the receipt in her jeans pocket, unties

her apron fast, drops it right there on the sidewalk, and runs toward her car in the lot behind the restaurant.

We follow her as she fumbles her keys and opens the driver's-side door. Then before she ducks in the car, she looks at us like she doesn't quite know what to do.

"We want to come," I say.

Oliver's mom exhales a hard breath that makes her lips sputter. Then she says, "Well, get in! Let's go!"

And I'm pretty sure that hopping in an adult's car in the middle of the day to drive over the speed limit to a bus station in another town breaks a thousand rules, but we already left school without telling anyone, and I don't see how we're just going to just walk back in there.

Plus, I want to find Oliver.

So Reuben and I squish in the back seat, and Oliver's mom says, "Sorry for the mess" and "Buckle up," but she doesn't wait to hear the click like my mom does before she backs the car out into the street, and I swear the tires screech as we take off down the road.

I'm sitting in the middle seat, squeezed in next to Reuben because there are boxes on the other side, and no one says anything for the first few minutes until we hit a red light and Oliver's mom stops quickly and slams her hands hard on the steering wheel. The clock in her car says that Oliver's bus departs in six minutes.

She's trying to call the bus station, and I'm

remembering my mom making a big deal about putting her phone out of sight while driving so she can be focused on the road, and I can see why now because Oliver's mom is swerving a little as she looks down to dial.

She puts it on speaker and drops the phone in her lap, but a robot keeps picking up and asking her to choose one, two, or three, but none of those options is about stopping Oliver's bus, so we listen to the staticky music play as we wait for an operator.

"We'll never make it," she says.

Then she looks left, and right, and waits for a car to pass in front of us, and then she just goes. She steps on the gas and we fly right through the red light. Cars are honking and she's yelling, "Sorry!" like they'll be able to hear. Or maybe she's yelling sorry to us because she takes off so fast that we are whipped back in our seats.

We come to another light but it's green, then it's yellow, but Oliver's mom steps on the gas and we speed through. We're passing a hundred cars in the other lane, and I'm wondering what the chances are that a cop will see us and turn on their lights before we reach the bus station.

Oliver's mom catches Reuben's eyes in the rearview mirror. "Shoot," she says. "I don't even think we've met." She passes another car. "God, what a mess. I'm Oliver's mom. Obviously."

"This is Reuben," I say.

Oliver's mom nods and pounds her hands on the wheel again as a car pulls out in front of her. "Friend from school?"

"Yeah," I say.

I feel my phone vibrate in my pocket, and I pull it out hoping it's Oliver but knowing it's my mom. That Ms. Leavitt caught on that we're missing, and she told Principal Tacker, and they called my mom, and now I'm waiting for Spider-Man to scale down from the roof of the car and snatch me back to the safety of the book-store.

Before I can even open the message, my phone buzzes with another one.

Gabe, where are you?

I'm worried sick.

Now she's calling, and I'm too nervous to pick up because I haven't exactly planned out what I'm going to say.

Then Reuben's phone starts buzzing too.

"My mom's freaking out," I say, looking down at my screen.

Reuben does that sign for *Me too.*

Oliver's mom is switching lanes and turning on her blinker to make a right-hand turn, but she says some-thing about calling our parents when we get there and how she should have called the school, but what a mess and we have to get to this bus, and we're running out of time.

My phone buzzes again.

This time it's not from my mom; it's a message from my dad, who doesn't normally text, especially right now because he should be sleeping before work, and it makes me feel extra nervous that I've been missing for only twenty-one minutes and the news has already woken him up.

Hey, Gabe. All OK?

"What are we going to tell them?" I ask.

Reuben shrugs, then types something into his phone and shows me the screen.

The truth, it says. *We haven't done anything wrong.*

And even though we've broken a hundred rules in the past twenty-one minutes, I think he's right, because I don't feel even the littlest bit of gobbledygook in my guts.

So I write back to my mom: *I'm safe. I have to help Oliver. I'm with his mom. I'll explain later, and you can ground me for 1,000 days if you have to.*

And then I send a message to my dad. *I'm OK. Oliver needs help and he's my best friend.*

My phone buzzes with another call from my mom, but I don't pick it up. Then it buzzes with two messages.

Maybe 999 days.

Be safe. See you in the morning.

It makes my eyes burn to think of Corn Pops with my dad, because even though I get to see him for a little bit each day, the missing is sometimes so deep. So I get it. I get why Oliver would want to sneak away, board a bus, and ride closer to his dad for another chance.

When we reach the bus station, Oliver's mom pulls into a parking spot crooked, tells us to stay here, leaves the car running, and sprints toward the front doors with the receipt from Ms. Leavitt's printer crumpled in one hand.

The clock says that we're three minutes too late, and it feels weird just sitting here and waiting and staring at the bus station door and hoping it flies back open and we see Oliver walking out.

The minute changes on the car's clock. Reuben is drumming his fingers on his knees.

Then I see the rack next to the entrance, and Oliver's bike is there, and even though Oliver's mom told us to wait here I unbuckle my seat belt, stretch over Reuben, and fling the door open.

"Come on," I say, and it takes Reuben half a second to reach into the driver's seat, turn the key, and pull it out of the ignition. Then we climb out and run to the station, and when we open the heavy door, we see Oliver's mom talking to a man at the ticket counter in the same voice she used in Principal Tacker's office—something about letting an unaccompanied minor board, and was he out of his mind?

"Call that bus back now," she says.

The man is already on the phone and clicking on the keyboard in front of him and saying that the ticket was purchased with a credit card online and that Oliver was checked in with a printed ticket at the gate.

There's a line forming behind Oliver's mom, and a guy at the back is shouting about how he's going to miss his bus and what is taking so long? Oliver's mom turns around, and I'm pretty sure she's about to tell him to shut his mouth and wait, but then she sees us and goes silent, and it's me who yells to the guy to wait his turn.

Then the man behind the desk asks Oliver's mom if those *unaccompanied minors* are supposed to be with her too.

"Shoot," she says. And she kind of collapses a little, her elbows catching on the counter in front of her, and she buries her head in her hands. "Just call that bus back," she says quietly, without looking up, like it's the last breath she has in her body.

The man tells her she can take a seat in the waiting area, and he'll call her when he gets through to the bus driver.

We rush to Oliver's mom and walk with her to the row of chairs, where we all sit down. There's a big window with two buses parked outside, both with lines of people who are holding out their tickets to a woman with a scanner and stepping inside. The guy who was shouting from the back of the line is finishing at the counter now and rushing out to catch his bus.

Oliver's mom hands me the bus receipt and takes out her phone. Her thumbs fly across the screen. "I'll tell him we're all waiting at the bus station," she says. "If he knows you're here, too, maybe he'll change his mind and tell the bus driver to turn around himself."

She shakes her head and says, "Why would he do this?" She sighs a big, loud sigh. "What was he thinking?"

The questions aren't for us, but I can't help trying to answer them in my head, and I'm pretty sure Reuben is, too, because we're kind of glancing at each other out of the corners of our eyes and pressing our lips into little frowns.

Oliver's mom is keeping her eyes on the man behind the desk, and we're all sitting with our elbows on our knees, holding our phones out in front of us, hoping they buzz with a message from Oliver.

28.

REUBEN

I KNOW WHAT OLIVER was thinking. That he could fix
something he thinks he broke.

29.

ANOTHER MINUTE GOES BY. If the bus left on time, Oliver is now twelve minutes down the road.

Oliver's mom is trying to call Oliver's dad, but it's going straight to voice mail. "We only ever talk through lawyers," she mumbles, hanging up again.

I have two more messages from my mom, and I text her that I'm still OK and I'll call her soon.

Then the man behind the counter calls over. "Ma'am? I got through."

Oliver's mom stands up.

"The bus is turning around now and due to arrive back in fourteen minutes."

She puts her hand over her heart and says, "Oh, thank God." Then she drops back to the chair.

My phone buzzes. This time it's from Oliver.

Is she mad?

I smile and type, *No.*

Then he writes a hundred questions like *How did she find out? Why are you with her? Is Reuben really there?*

So I scooch over closer to Reuben, and I gesture to Oliver's mom to squish in, and I stretch my arm out as far as I can to get us all in a picture that I send to Oliver.

We're all here, I write.

It's silent for the next few minutes as we wait, but then his mom says, "He was working way past bedtime last night on that comic you're making." I look up at her. "I was late that day you stayed with him on the teeter-totter," she says, and shakes her head. "It was the first day of school."

I smile. "And now he's my best friend."

Reuben pats my knee, and I hate that the first thing I think of is that if Chaz saw that he might still laugh, because really, it feels good, that pat. It feels like he's saying that I'm a good friend. So I smile and pat his hand that's patting my knee, and I hope he knows that I'm telling him that he's a good friend too.

And I really do hope Chaz can quit it. Quit making fun, so he can have a real friend like Oliver too. A real friend like Reuben.

"I know his dad was supposed to pick him up that

day," I say to Oliver's mom.

She looks at me. "He remembers that?"

I nod. "And he thinks that what happened in fourth grade, you know, his dad leaving, was his fault."

"No," she says, and shakes her head. "No. Oliver knows that his dad was so excited for him. From the moment I was pregnant . . ."

"That's why he thinks it's his fault," I say. "He knows his dad was excited and that he really wanted a boy." I take a breath. "But then he left anyway."

His mom's eyes fill, and she wipes the tears away with her sleeve. "Shoot," she says.

Then I pat her knee and say, "I'll let Oliver tell you the rest."

We see a bus pull up outside through the big windows. It stops and opens its door and gives out a big hissing sigh. No one gets off for a minute; then Oliver, with his book bag and sports bag hanging off his arms, nods to the bus driver and steps down.

We all stand, and his mom runs out and pulls Oliver into a hug. We're watching from the big window as she waves to the bus driver and calls out, "Thank you."

Then she stands in front of Oliver and puts both her hands on his arms. She points right at his heart, and I can see from here Oliver's shoulders start to shake, and he's crying. And I'm thinking back and back and wondering if I've ever seen him cry before, not the laugh-so-hard-we-cry kind of cry and not little-escape-tears kind of cry, but a good, hard cry, and the answer is no. And I'm hoping it feels good, like he's letting something go or dropping something heavy.

When they come back inside the station, Oliver looks at us and waves. I pull the paper receipt out of my pocket and say, "We found this in Ms. Leavitt's printer. That's too easy a clue for Gabiver."

He laughs and puts his hands up like we caught him. His eyes are still wet, and he's not trying to wipe the tears away. Then he pulls a piece of paper from his book bag and holds it out. It's a flyer for a whole-town bas-ketball tournament on the center green in a little town called Troivo in Massachusetts. There's a schedule on the side with times for all sorts of games: seniors, youth, high school. Father-son.

"I started looking up Troivo, just wondering what's so great about it." He shrugs like the town didn't seem so special after all. "Then I saw this," he says, and hands his mom the tournament flyer. "And I knew he'd be here. He never missed watching any local games. Even little-kid rec leagues."

Then he looks up at his mom. "I thought I would sur-prise him, show up, and if he could see me now, how good I've gotten, maybe he'd want to play with me. Maybe

242

he'd want to come back. Then we could keep our house, you could drop a shift, and things would be easier." He shakes his head. "It was stupid."

His mom hugs him. "It's not stupid," she says. "It's thoughtful, and incredible, and everything you are." She squeezes him tight. "But it wouldn't have worked."

Oliver sniffs, and his mom says right in his ear, "Because he didn't leave because of you. He left because of him."

Oliver straightens up, and his mom shakes her head and wipes away a tear on her cheek. Then she says, "And things might not be easy right now, but that's not because of him leaving or because of you. It's just because."

Now Reuben is wiping a tear from his cheek, and we pull Oliver into a four-person hug, and I tell him we're glad that the bus turned around and that he's OK. Oliver nods and lets us squeeze our arms around him before he says, "OK, OK. Let's get out of here."

"Yeah," I say, "because I might be in quite a bit of guano with my mom."

We all laugh and link up our arms and head out of the bus station toward the parking lot, Oliver right in the middle of Reuben and me, and that feels good.

30.

REUBEN

I'M TRYING TO REMEMBER what Oliver's mom said.

Repeating it over and over in my head.

Some things are hard and awful just because.

Just because.

The rain froze and glazed our playground just because. I was telling a superhero story just because. Our teacher was listening to me with all her attention just because.

He slipped. He *slipped*.

And the doctors couldn't save him just because.

It wasn't the doctors. It wasn't the rain. It wasn't me.

It was just because. A hard, awful just because.

31.

MY MOM DOESN'T GROUND me for 999 days. She
doesn't even say that I can't go on the backpacking trip
this summer. She only says that she's glad that Oliver is
home and that she's proud of me for being there for him.

And then, after I've called Dad and explained the
whole thing, she does something that surprises the scat
right out of me.

She says yes when I ask if I can sleep over at Oliver's
house. On a school night.

I tell her it's to finish our comic because it's due
tomorrow and we missed working on it today. But it's
mostly because I just want to be there with my friend.

So I pack a change of clothes, my toothbrush, and a
few extra colored pencils in my book bag. Then I toss a

carrot nub in Puppy's cage and tell her I'll take her for a plastic-exercise-ball roll tomorrow, but right now I have a friend to see and a comic to finish.

Mom turns off the car and comes with me to the front door. And it nearly surprises the scat right out of me *again* when Reuben answers the door with Oliver.

"We have to finish our comic," Oliver says. "Get in here already."

I introduce my mom to Reuben, and then I give her a big hug and tell her I'll see her tomorrow, and I don't even say anything when she calls me *honey.*

"Text me when you're going to bed," she says, and I agree as Oliver pulls me into the house.

Then my mom and Oliver's mom sit out on their front step for a while, talking, while we lay out the frames for *Gabiver and the Leave-No-Trace Mission.*

I finish the speech and thought bubbles in the hiking scene. I even make one of the squirrels Oliver drew in the trees say, *Thanks, Gabiver!* And one bubbles up from the fish in the stream. *You saved our gills!*

Then in the last frame, on the playground, where Gabiver stands between the bully and the other kid, Gabiver says, *I think we can quit it. Quit being mean.*

"This is good," Oliver says. "Really good."

I look through the whole thing and nod, and Reuben traces his fingers across the final drawing of the playground. Then he takes my black colored pencil and makes a thought bubble coming up from his character, who is taking one step away from the bricks of the building: *One tiny step*, it says.

Then I say, "You know what? This feels like a series to me." And I open my notebook to a blank piece of paper. "I'm thinking in the next chapter there's another big collision scene where Gabiver crashes into . . . Reuben!"

Reuben smiles and laughs.

"And in order to save them, they need to be sewn into thirds!" Oliver says.

"Reugabiver!" I shout. "A sporty, bookish, excellent listener, who's a crime-solving machine!"

"And Reugabiver's first mission?" Oliver does a drumroll on the edge of the table and says, "To rise up against Principal Tacker's cell phone policy."

"Or to restore the graphic novels back to their rightful place in Rae's English class!"

We all laugh, and Reuben's eyes fill a little with tears, and they seem like the kind of tears that spill from laughing too hard or from being really happy. I reach out my fist for bumps, and we all connect in the middle.

We spend the rest of the night eating string cheese and talking about the latest Dog Man book and taking runs down the basement stairs on our duct-taped piece of cardboard until Oliver's mom says it's time to go to bed.

Reuben and I make two nests on Oliver's floor the way I used to, out of extra blankets and pillows and stuffed animals, and Oliver and I explain to Reuben about our summer backpacking trip.

"We'll sleep in a tent," Oliver says. "And climb two tall peaks. And we'll have to filter all our water so we don't get sick, and hang our food from special bags in a tree so bears don't get it, and bring this padded tape stuff to wrap around our blisters."

I'm hearing Oliver's excitement build and trying not to second-guess this trip. Actually, by this point it's probably third- or seventh-guessing. But then I tell them what I've learned in Nature Club. How to follow a path and recover when you get lost, and how to work as a team.

"And how to poop in the woods?" Oliver says.

"I still don't have any idea how to do that!" I say.

We all laugh, and Reuben reaches for his phone on the floor near his head. The screen glows on his face while he looks something up, and then he turns his phone around to show us a video of a guy modeling how to walk far off the trail, dig a hole, then get into "hug a tree" position to poop.

"Then you have to bury it," Oliver says.

We're all laughing so hard we can't stop, and we

hear two loud knocks on Oliver's bedroom door. "Bedtime, boys. It's a school night."

And that just makes us giggle more, so we hide our heads under our pillows to muffle the sounds.

And when the room finally quiets, I whisper, "You should come with us, Reuben."

"Yes!" Oliver says. "I know my uncle Toby would say yes."

Reuben exhales, and I'm thinking about him watching us like a guard from the brick wall of the school while we swing and slide and play. Wondering if he would find it scary in the woods or whether putting out one foot, then the other, down the trail might feel OK.

"It would be awesome," I whisper. "And if *my* mom said yes, I'm one thousand percent sure that your mom will too."

That makes Oliver giggle a little into his pillow.

And after a few more minutes of silence I whisper toward Reuben's nest on the floor, "Just think about it."

And I'm pretty sure if I could read all our thought bubbles, they'd say something like, *Together, we can do this.*

The next day, Ms. Leavitt has our room set up for our project gallery walk. We all arrange our projects on the tables, and Ms. Leavitt instructs us to make a paper tent with the project's title and the authors. I write out *Gabiver and the Leave-No-Trace Mission* and *By Gabe Mackey and Oliver Quick*. Then I add *And Reuben Tanner*, even though Reuben has his own project that he's setting up on the table near the library.

When everyone is ready Ms. Leavitt says we can visit our classmates' projects now, and to jot a positive comment on their comment sheets.

Oliver and I leave the comic spread out across our table and head to Cass's desk, where there's a laptop with a recording of her playing the song she wrote. She's taped a copy of the lyrics and the sheet music to the desk. It's a song about her little sister. The chorus rhymes, and it's clear, when you watch Cass's face, that she's proud of her sister and the song.

I write on the comment sheet that she's a great writer and performer.

I see Missy and Tanya's clay scene. They made a baseball field with all the players and a ball suspended in midair by a thin piece of wire heading toward the home run wall in the outfield. The batter is taking off toward first base, her fist in the air.

Then I get to Chaz's diorama, and it looks kind of like it looked when he was working on it. Like a winter boots box with messy shreds of paper hanging from holes punched through the ceiling. But when I look closer and move some of the long shreds of hanging paper, I see a little figure made of tinfoil covered up by all the scraps.

I'm about to look up and ask him, "What the heck?" when I pull my hand back out and realize the shreds hanging from the top of the box, almost burying the figure, are made up of old practice tests with multiple-choice answer bubbles penciled in, and the whole inside of the box is wallpapered with essay responses to reading tests.

The title in front of the box says, *Paper Weight*.

And I'm wondering what that's supposed to mean until Reuben shows up next to me and his hands find the tinfoil figure inside the box, too, smothered by test answers. He reads the wallpaper and runs his fingers down the strips of multiple choice. Then he exhales and looks down and writes on the comment sheet, *That must be hard.*

And then I get it. All that *gifted* and testing and extra is a lot of pressure. And maybe that's why he sometimes acts the way he does, and maybe it's not. But it still reminds me that everyone's carrying their own hard stuff.

Thanks for sharing this, I write on his comment sheet. Then I see Oliver moving to Reuben's table, so I go and stand there next to him.

Reuben's project is a full-page spread of the comic he's been drawing on the jagged paper. On the left side, the smooth-edged side, is a picture of him with a thousand full-to-the-brim speech bubbles. Superhero stories about magical capes and Spidey senses. About curing the sick and saving the troubled. "Look at me!" some of them say. "Listen to me!"

Then the middle of the page is a huge cartoon-explosion *POW* with lightning bolts and stars, and underneath, if you really squint and get close, you can see a scene, drawn lightly, on a playground. Reuben with a thousand speech bubbles, tugging on his teacher's jacket. A kid flying from the jungle gym.

Then on the right side of the paper, it's Reuben again, pressed against the brick of the school wall, this time with a thousand thought bubbles. *If I could just help*, one says. *If I could just be quiet. Still. Watch. Listen.* Then the page fades out with its jagged edge.

Reuben's standing off to the side, and I look up. "Something happened," I say, pressing my hand to the middle of his comic. "On a playground." He nods.

And I think back to fourth grade, a few towns over, and the team of workers who came to assess our playground the next week. They dumped wood chips and measured their thickness and dumped more and measured again. They wrapped foam pads around the corners of the jungle gym, hammered No Running signs into the ground, and hung whistles around the recess aides' necks.

And I have a hundred questions about what exactly happened beneath the *POW* that changed Reuben from speech bubbles to thought bubbles, but I know it's hard.

I'm here, I write on his comment sheet.

Me too, Oliver writes.

Then I look at Reuben and say, "And if you ever want to talk about it, or if you never do. We're just . . . here."

He nods and smiles a little and steps over to stand a little closer to us.

And as I'm looking out at all our projects, about little sisters, and best friends, and first home runs, and heavy pressures, and big, hard, terrible moments, I'm thinking about all the things we carry in our guts, and I'm thinking who gives a guano about cool points? We all have enough of those, all on our own.

And I'm also thinking that there's no such thing as *leave no trace*. Because we do. We leave traces on everyone we meet. It's just what kind of trace we leave that matters. Are we going to be a piece of plastic stuck in a tree where a bird was trying to make its nest? Or are we a seed dropped so something new can grow tall and strong and add more oxygen to the world, making it easier to breathe?

Ms. Leavitt says time is up and calls us all to stand in a circle around the projects. She tells us the things teachers always say when we finish a big project like this. She's proud of us. She loves watching us grow, watching us create. But this time, I feel it too. I feel like I've made something. Something real.

I've tightened the stitches of my friendship with Oliver, and I've opened them up enough to invite Reuben in.

I've learned how to speak when it's important, and how to listen.

Epilogue.

SUMMER

WHEN WE SEE THE trailhead, Dad pulls the car to the side of the road and puts on the flashers. My mom is in the front seat because even though it doesn't take two parents to drop off one hiker, she insisted on coming, and so did my dad, so here we all are.

Mom turns around and looks me over from breathable hiking cap to fancy dry-wicking shirt to hiking boots that tie up over my ankles. "You sure about this?" she asks.

I nod. "Positive."

"Timber rattlesnake?" she reminds me.

"Still endangered," I say.

She laughs and reaches back to tap the brim of my

cap. Then she nods toward my door. "Be careful getting out," she says.

I wait for a truck to pass by before I open my door quickly and hustle around to the back of the car. I lean on the bumper and tighten the laces of my boots. Mom and Dad lean next to me.

"Remember what Oliver's uncle said," I tell them. "We won't get service everywhere, so if you don't hear from us, that's why."

"Well, I'll have to *assume* that's why," Mom says.

I roll my eyes, and she nudges me. "OK, OK, I won't worry."

Then Reuben's car pulls up behind us, and I can see him sitting in the front passenger seat.

"I'm really glad he's joining you," Dad says.

I nod. "Me too."

Reuben's car stops, and his mom unbuckles her belt and turns around in her seat. I'm pretty sure she's telling Knox and Kobe to stay still and she'll just be a minute. Reuben opens his door, and I can hear the twins giggling and screaming. I would give them lollipops.

Reuben gets out and waves, and we wave back.

"You ready for this?" I say. He smiles big and shakes his head.

"Me either." I laugh.

Then Oliver's mom pulls up behind Reuben's car, and Oliver opens the back-seat door as soon as they stop. Uncle Toby gets out, too, and all our moms make a little triangle around him, asking him questions that he's already answered a hundred times about the route and blisters and bug spray.

Dad opens the trunk and helps me get my pack out. Then Oliver, Reuben, and I get together and rub sunscreen on the backs of our necks and up our arms.

"You didn't chicken out!" Oliver says.

I laugh and tell him to quit it, but really I'm thinking he's not far off, because after we packed our hiking backpacks with his uncle last week, splitting the food, and the tent poles, and the rain fly, and the first aid and blister kits, and bear bags for our food, and after we slid extra granola bars into the side pockets because Toby assured us we'd need the calories, and sealed folded squares of toilet paper in Ziploc bags, I wasn't so sure I didn't want to just stay home and read.

But after we filled our water bladders, and weighed our packs, and practiced cinching the belts around our hips, I think Oliver could hear all that doubt in my guts because he put his hands right on my hiking-packed shoulders and said, "It's going to be awesome."

Reuben clips the strap across his chest and puts his

fist out for a bump. And I know when it comes to finding a path and staying true to your compass, these guys are the realest deal.

The moms all remind Toby to be in touch when he can, and after we wave goodbye to Knox and Kobe through their back window, and after Mom pulls me in by the straps and hugs me right around my whole hiking pack and definitely calls me *honey*, we take our first step onto the trail.

And I'm thinking if you lined up a thousand kids, I wouldn't take one step of a thirty-five-mile hike with 998 of them, but Reuben is number 999, and Oliver is number one thousand.

ACKNOWLEDGMENTS

GABE'S VOICE CAME TO me during a very hard year for our country, for our world. We were sheltering-in from a global pandemic. We were scared, uncertain, and grieving the loss of so many lives and jobs and connections. We were angry and broken over the murder of George Floyd. We were divided and searching for hope.

At times this book felt impossible to write. And one time, before I ever even really began, I quit. I told my husband, Kamahnie, I was giving up for now, that it was too much to manage while caring for our young children and filtering for them the weight of the world. He handed me the dog's leash, and I knew what it meant: *Go listen to Gabe's voice. Sort it out.* I'm so grateful for that walk. It turned out to be hours, and it ended in a breathless monologue to him about how I was going to do it. I leaned on Kamahnie so many times throughout this book, and it simply wouldn't be without him.

To my editor, Erica Sussman, you helped me strengthen the heartbeat of this story in the sharp, succinct, magical way you always do. Thank you for the time and care you spent on each draft so that readers can clearly see how powerful a friendship can be, how important it is to listen, to find your voice, and to pay attention to what's in your guts. I'm so thankful for the whole team at HarperCollins, including Stephanie Guerdan, Jessica Berg, Gwen Morton, Catherine Lee, Alison Donalty, Vanessa Nuttry, Vaishali Nayak, and Aubrey Churchward, who have been so supportive in making this story a book. Special thanks also to Maike Plenzke for the gorgeous cover and back cover, bringing Gabe, Oliver, and Reuben to life.

And my agent, Stephen Barbara, who always reminds me that I've written a special story. I appreciate how much you support each book, and the time you have invested in helping me build a career as a writer for children. And, if you lined up a thousand agents, 999 wouldn't go on a weeks-long text-and-email rally to find the perfect title. But you are number one thousand.

Lauren Catherwood-Ginn, Jen Ochoa, and Jess

Rothenberg, you are my lifelines, and I never, ever feel far from you.

And to the first responders and essential workers, to those who stayed home, and those who masked and marched, and vaccinated and raised their voices, and everyone who did as much as they could to contribute to our public health. And to the educators, the educators, the educators, and the students, the students, the students . . .

Thank you.

And to Miles and Paige, this marks the fifth and final book I will write with you in my belly, on my chest, at my feet, on my lap, and as you play. As I type now, you are beginning your first days of kindergarten and preschool, your own adventures into education and friendships and finding your brave and following what's deep inside you and building your own teams who will lift you up and support you along your way.

We've had quite a book-writing run, you two. You are on every page.